Pestilence:
A Medieval Tale of Plague

by Jeani Rector

THE ABBOT.

(From Holbein's " Dance of Death.")

THE 'DANCE OF DEATH.'

THE PEDLAR.

Pestilence:
A Medieval Tale of Plague

by Jeani Rector

Ring around the rosie;
Pockets full of posies.
Ashes, ashes
We all fall down!

—14th Century nursery rhyme

THE
HORROR ZINE

Published by The Horror Zine Books

**THE
HORROR ZINE**

Edited by Dean H. Wild
Bat art created by Riaan Marais

Cover and Interior Design By
Stephen James Price
www.BookLooksDesign.com

Published by The Horror Zine Books
www.thehorrorzine.com

Introduction

As appalling as it may seem, the storyline in this novel describes real events that occurred in the 14th Century. Almost all the depictions in this book about life in medieval times and about the bubonic plague are factual and are historically accurate. The very few instances that are not accurately described are outlined in the back of this book under *Author's Note About Creative Liberty*.

Only the individual characters, including Elaisse Sheffield, are fictional. This book is intended to represent what life might have been like during the plague years as seen through the eyes of someone who could have lived through the experience.

In *Pestilence: A Medieval Tale of Plague*, great care was taken to realistically portray the destruction of human life as a direct result of the bubonic plague, including the descriptions as to the cause and symptoms of the illness according to modern studies and scientific findings.

Care was also taken to insure that the characters never referred to the illness as "The Black Death," as that term was not used until the 16th Century. During the time period of this novel, the bubonic plague was simply known as "the pestilence," and the deaths due to it were called "The Great Dying."

This brings us to the issue of dialogue.

In *Pestilence: A Medieval Tale of Plague*, the speech of the characters is modern, and not the Olde English actually spoken in the 14th Century. This is done for the ease of the reader and to move the storyline along smoothly. In reality, the contrast of speech today and that which was spoken in medieval times is so great that it could almost be considered a different language, even though technically it is not.

So, although creative license is taken in very rare instances, again it must be stressed that almost all events depicted in this book were real and are accurately described.

There truly were flagellants between the years of 1346-1350, who were extreme penitents that believed their personal suffering would take God's attention away from His intent to punish the rest of the world. The men who pushed carts through the streets and cried, "Bring out your dead!" were also real, because the populations perished in such great numbers that out of necessity, drastic measures were taken for body removal.

It is difficult in this day and age to imagine the superstitions of the 14th Century, but in absence of scientific facts, the people did their best to deal with the horror of the circumstances by explaining it to themselves in any way they could. The ideas that they concocted to explain, and especially to prevent the disease, would seem ridiculous by today's standards, but were very convincing to the people of medieval times.

The religious beliefs described in this book should be mentioned. Although mostly a Protestant country today, medieval England was Catholic during the 14th Century. It was not until the reign of King Henry VIII that the Church of England was formed and the country became Protestant.

The portrayals of religion in this book are not necessarily any reflection of the author's personal beliefs or convictions, but are accurate depictions of the beliefs and convictions of the medieval people. Both the love of God and the fear of God were prominent in the 14th Century, and the devotion and fervor to religious beliefs were passionately embraced during that time period in history.

Certainly the bubonic plague must have tested the faith of the medieval people in the most extreme fashion, and this is reflected by the contemplations of Elaisse Sheffield during the story.

Pestilence: A Medieval Tale of Plague opens with the character Elaisse as an innocent but self-centered sixteen-year-old of royal heritage who is suddenly thrust into a changing world. Circumstances arise beyond her control and she goes from a structured, sheltered life into one where normalcy falls by the wayside. This book demonstrates Elaisse's change from a foolish child into a wise, mature woman who finds a way to deal with the unprecedented mass destruction of human life that surrounds her.

Yersinia pestis and the resulting incidences of bubonic plague still exist to this day. However, fortunately for modern mankind, the illness is caused by a bacterium and not a virus. Therefore, plague can be halted by antibiotics so it is no longer a life-threatening illness if treated. So far, *Yersinia pestis* has not become antibiotic-resistant. So far.

Today there are many end-of-the-world tales, but the bubonic plague pandemic in the 14th Century is the original apocalypse story.

THE 'DANCE OF DEATH.'

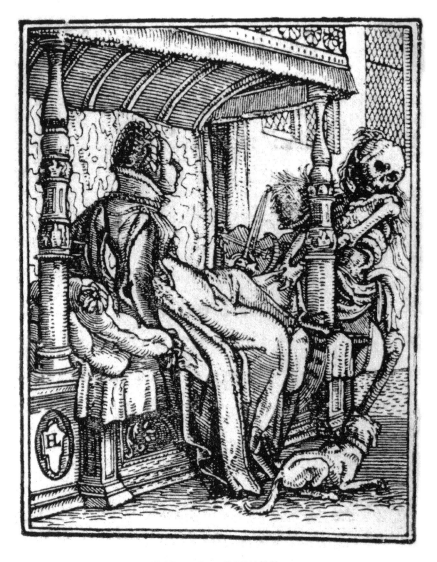

THE DUCHESS.

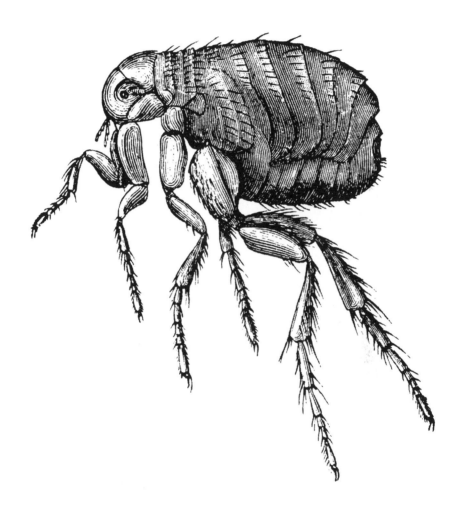

Chapter One

The flea was hungry.

Its flattened body, similar in shape to a sunfish, made for easy maneuvering through the hair shafts. Because its large hind legs were adapted for jumping, the flea could travel quickly, with the ability to leap seven inches vertically and thirteen inches horizontally. It had a row of spines that could catch the hair with a backward pull, so it would not be easily dislodged if its host attempted to scratch it off.

With its rows of sharp mandibles, the flea bit into the flesh of its victim, but the flea's bite went unnoticed until salivary secretions caused an itching sensation in the rat. Even though it had just punctured the skin of the unfortunate host to extract its meal of blood, the flea was still hungry.

This flea was infected with *Yersinia pestis*, a bacterium that, in the quantities multiplying within its system, created a blockage in its throat. When the flea attempted to feed, the meal could not pass below the blockage. Instead, the flea regurgitated the blood back into the rat because it was unable to swallow.

The rat only received its own blood back after more *Yersinia pestis* was added from the flea's system. The flea would eventually starve to death. The host received the regurgitated blood containing the bacterium, and would inevitably die of the disease the bacterium caused. The flea and the rat were the original vectors in an event of horrific magnitude, because the bubonic plague had arrived in medieval England.

September 1348

Elaisse sat in front of her looking glass, studying the face reflected back at her. The brushing she had just given her hair caused the golden tresses to fall around her white shoulders in waves. She knew that vanity was a sin, but she was secretly glad she was pretty. Gazing at her large, gray-blue eyes, Elaisse noticed a couple of hairs growing from her eyebrows that had, just days earlier it seemed, been fiercely plucked. Sighing, she reached for the tweezers. She winced as she removed any wayward hairs she found, leaving a smooth, hairless brow. No matter how painful it was to pluck, this was the fashion.

"You might want to pull out some of the head hair gowning at your forehead," suggested Fern, the maid. "After all, the larger the forehead, the more beautiful the lady."

"No," Elaisse said, "the nebule on my head-dress will cover the top of my forehead so it won't matter. Would you help me braid my hair? Oh, and I want to wear my embroidered dress today. Could you get it for me please?"

Fern rushed to get the dress. Bringing it to her mistress, she said, "This dress will certainly impress the knights at the tournament. It's cut low, so it will accentuate your long neck. I'll bet John of Essex notices you today."

Elaisse blushed, for she would be seventeen in December, and she knew it was time she married. She had confided to Fern about her secret admiration of John Wythe. John was twenty, and had recently become a knight. Elaisse was thinking about how his dark eyes would crinkle when he smiled. She dreamily imagined him standing tall and straight in the room before her, his brown hair falling down to his neck, his chin strong and jutting, and his broad shoulders tapering into a thin waist.

She felt a thrill ripple through her body as she thought of his touch. She suddenly trembled as she recaptured in her mind details of the last time she had seen him. Elaisse had secretly met with John in the stable, stealthily creeping into the night for a forbidden encounter. Although he had wanted to lay in the straw with her, she had put limits on his desires. Would she let him explore more of her body the next time they met? The idea was both abhorrent yet incredibly tantalizing.

She liked to think about her meetings with John and to envisage future meetings. She scripted potential interactions between her and John in her mind over and over again, each time imagining different twists in her little fantasy plays so that the outcome was never the same from one day to the next. But in real life, Elaisse knew that she would never permit her fantasies to completely materialize unless she and John were married. Still, she wondered if she dared to give John a little peek at herself the next time they met.

I'll see John at today's tournament, Elaisse thought. She took special care in the way she dressed because she wanted to insure that John would notice her. She inched into her dress, and when it was positioned properly, she pushed the bodice down to reveal the tops of her small breasts. She tucked her braids up into her headpiece, which was a soft tan color, enhanced by gold stitching and a veil that covered her ears and gathered at the back of her neck.

When she met her parents outside by the carriage, her father scowled at her. "I don't like what you've got on," William told her. "That dress is too low at the bust. You're too young to wear it."

She anticipated this reaction from her father, which was why she had dallied so long to get dressed. She wanted to make sure that it would be too late for him to insist that she go back and change. She knew her father would never want to miss even a second of the day's events. She took a chance and said, "I can go back and change, but that would take a long time."

"No, it's too late now. Get in the carriage," William ordered, and Elaisse smiled inwardly. How well she knew her father.

Even though the jousting field was close to the castle, she rode in the carriage with her father and her mother, the Lady Hildred. The carriage heaved as it bumped along the hardpan dirt of the road that lay between the castle and the neighboring village. She knew that her family was to be a proper and fitting example to the peasants who lived in the village, so although the field lay within walking distance between the castle and the village, William insisted they ride.

"Who will be there?" Elaisse asked her father, although she already knew. Pretending to be innocent was everything.

"Only the nobility from Essex County are invited to this tournament," William said. "This is a formal event, with no peasants allowed. We need to make a good impression on our neighbors from Essex. Peasants would only drag the dirt and filth from the fields into the stands, and their ignorant ways would be an embarrassment, so of course they won't be in attendance."

Elaisse never spent much time with peasants, having no reason to be exposed to them, but she listened to her father's demoralization of the lower class with only one ear. Young enough to be an idealist, she privately thought that her father never had a kind word to say about most people in general, so she frequently ignored his opinions. Still, she loved her father fiercely. It was a paradox that she couldn't understand.

But there was something else on her mind this morning besides the tournament, and even besides her fantasies about John Wythe. She had been hearing the servants gossip among themselves about something that worried her. While she had his attention in the confines of the small carriage, she decided to ask her father about what was bothering her.

"I heard the servants talking about a great pestilence in France," Elaisse said. "They say it's rampant, and that a lot of people are sick, even dying. Daddy, do you know anything about it?"

"I've heard talk, but it's all nonsense!" William exclaimed. "You've no reason to fear. Isn't England gaining control over France? Didn't King Edward III just win an easy victory in Sluys, Crecy, and Calais? That shows you how incredibly weak the French people are. They have no fortitude, so of course they get sick! If the French people are diseased, then they should give penance for their sins, because God does not approve of their resistance to England's rightful claims. God is punishing the French so that they will see the error of their ways."

Elaisse persisted. "Still, Daddy, I can't help but overhear what the servants are saying. Even Fern said something about it. She told me that this pestilence came out of Cathay by ships that made landfall in France. She's afraid because the port in Suffolk is so near Wynham Castle."

"We'll have no more talk of this," William said. "How dare you listen to the ignorance of peasants? Servants don't know their place any more. Don't be as uneducated as they are by giving any credence to their tales. And you treat Fern like a friend instead of the maid that she is. You need to keep a firm hand with servants so that they do not forget their lot in life."

"I like Fern," Elaisse whispered quietly, but no one heard. She was thinking that she had no friends other than a maid.

Her father changed the subject. "I wish Henry were here for this. I'd like to see him perform in the jousting match."

Elaisse silently considered her brother Henry, who was two years older than herself. She thought, *Henry looks a lot like me, but he's not like me at all. I would never admit this out loud, but I hope he stays in military training for a long time.*

Quickly the carriage arrived at the field that would hold the war games. Elaisse saw that anticipation had everyone giddy, and she let herself be carried away with the excitement of the crowd, shutting the servants' gossip into a compartment at the back of her mind.

The seats were filled to capacity, but special places had been saved for Elaisse's noble family. In the stands, the wealth of the people in attendance was obvious. Everyone was brilliantly dressed, and the vivid colors of their clothing swam in waves of constant movement as people enthusiastically waved flags and blew horns. Ribbons fluttered as the ladies threw them down towards favored knights. The noise of the crowd escalated into a loud clamoring as the first round of knights emerged onto the field below.

Elaisse thought, *How my everyday life pales in comparison to this!*

Below on the ground, great ceremony was observed as the knights chose their opponents, bowing to the crowd and delighting in the admiration they received. Elaisse was awed by the energy that seemed to radiate from everyone around her. Even the horses appeared to feel the excitement as the muscled steeds pranced and snorted, draped in colorful fighting gear.

The simulated battle between knights from different regions began in earnest. Opponents were chosen, and each knight suited up in complete fighting gear: helmets, chain neck-guards, body armor, and metal footwear. She knew that all knights wore linen padding under their helmets to muffle any blows; otherwise, if a sword struck the metal helmet, the resulting *clang* would be deafening.

On the ground, knights charged at break-neck speed towards each other, knocking one another off their steeds with long, blunt-ended poles. When one knight was overthrown, another immediately took over. Defeated knights were captured and held for ransom back to their lords, sometimes in exchange for horses, sometimes for armor. It was all in great, raucous fun, and it was a way for the knights to show off to the public and bask in its glory, at least for the winners. The defeated lost not only the mock battle, but their pride as well.

Elaisse held her breath when she saw John Wythe ride onto the field with the knights from Essex. This time, two groups of knights were to ride against each other, five in each group. The noise was deafening when the riders impacted against each other, their spikes cracking, and their armor crashing.

Suddenly something went very wrong. A young knight was knocked from the saddle and began to fall from his horse. His metal shoe caught in the stirrup, leaving him dangling dangerously, still attached to his mount. The young knight tried to pull himself up, but was unable to grasp the saddle and couldn't find the reins. The horse, already pumped with adrenaline and spooked from the strange behavior of the rider, bolted across the field.

The stands grew abruptly silent, and then a collective gasp went through the crowd. The young knight was dragged helplessly by his running horse. Time stopped, and so did the other knights on the field. Suddenly one of the riders turned his mount to chase the runaway horse as an attempt to intercept it. Others followed suit and broke into action to stop the young knight's horse.

John Wythe was in the lead of the thundering group of knights chasing the runaway horse. He caught up with the fleeing mount, and reached to grasp the reins that were flapping in the wind. The young knight, still helplessly dragged, was unconscious, probably very badly hurt if not already dead. Leaning out of his saddle at a dangerous angle as his own horse raced forward, John was able to grab the reins of the young knight's runaway mount. John pulled back on the reins, and the knight's horse shook his head violently, but slowed down. John pulled the runaway horse to a stop.

The crowd suddenly came to life, screaming and cheering. Horns blew, and multitudes of ribbons came fluttering down along with material ripped from sleeves to show their support. The crowd was ecstatic. What a show!

John remained on his own horse, holding the reins of the trembling and frothing young knight's horse. The other knights leaped from their mounts to assess the damage to the victim.

"He's alive!" exclaimed one of the knights at the top of his voice, and all around Elaisse, the crowd went even wilder. They screamed and banged on the seats. It became pandemonium as spectators rushed onto the field to touch John, to pound him on the back, and to shake his hand. John's mount reared up, and other knights pushed the spectators back.

"Go to your seats!" cried one of the knights in the circle surrounding John. Slowly the crowd moved off, and the knights were able to carry the injured young man off the field.

Elaisse watched it all from the stands, barely able to contain her excitement. Surely the bravery of John Wythe would impress her father. He might even consider this act worthy enough to allow John her hand in marriage.

When her father was distracted, she slipped from her seat and made her way into the crowd. She knew that once her absence was discovered she would be punished, but she felt she had to talk to John, no matter what the consequences.

The crowd was festive, and contained high classes of people from both Suffolk and Essex counties, from nobility to merchants and artisans. Elaisse carefully stepped down from the stands. Never venturing far from the castle before, she was unprepared for the contrast of the good humor of some people, and the rude mannerisms of others. She didn't want to shove people out of her way, but he crowd was caught up in the excitement of the moment and she was constantly blocked as people failed to let her pass. Still, she was determined to find John, so she firmly pushed people aside, continuously saying 'excuse me' to deaf ears.

She spotted John off the field as he gave his horse into a servant's care. It was the incentive she needed, so she became assertive and elbowed her way through the unyielding crowd.

John grinned as Elaisse approached and said, "I'll bet my saddle that your father doesn't know where you are."

"Keep your saddle," she said, "because of course Daddy doesn't know. But I didn't come to talk to you about my father. Oh, John, you were wonderful! You made me so proud. You are the bravest knight in all the county!"

The corners of John's brown eyes crinkled as he smiled. "Go back to your seat," he said loudly for the benefit of bystanders. Then he whispered one word: *Tonight*.

Her heart raced. She nodded. She understood the message. Then she turned to go back up the stands to where her parents were seated.

"Where have you been?" demanded William as she sat beside him once again.

Elaisse forced herself to look her father directly in the eye. "I went to congratulate John Wythe. His courage is extraordinary. Daddy, he's the man I want to marry."

William's face darkened. "We've been over this before. You are promised to Sir Geoffrey Gladden, Lord of Framlingham."

"Oh Daddy! Sir Geoffrey is too old. He's almost as old as you are."

The blood rose to William's cheeks. "Geoffrey's wife has died, God rest her soul, so now we've been given this opportunity. He is looking for another wife. It's been agreed that land is to be exchanged between our families when this marriage takes place. There is to be no argument from you! How spoiled you are. A girl's fancy comes and goes with every whim. But marriage is serious business, and you will be the lady of the castle at Framlingham. That's high status indeed, not to mention the land that will be added to my estate with the merging of our bloodlines. As his wife, you will be held in high regard. About John Wythe, he may be a knight, but his family owns no property, so he'll be lucky if he rises to the rank of earl. And, as far as age goes, there's still a lot of life in someone my age."

Was there nothing Elaisse could do? She could not imagine herself married to Sir Geoffrey, held in bondage to a man who was reputed to be mean-tempered and cruel. But she knew it was true that the farmland held by the Framlingham castle was fertile. In these seasons of unusually heavy rains and frequent crop failures, obtaining some of the Framlingham land could save Wynham from the lean times it had been experiencing as of late.

Well, she thought, *I'm not married yet.* She was determined to find a way to meet John Wythe later that night in the castle's stables.

When evening came, Elaisse sat on her bed. She looked around her bedroom that was so familiar to her after so many years. The bed was curtained, and the pillows were feather-filled linen. Off to the side of the bedchamber was an anteroom where the maid was to sleep, positioned to ensure that Fern would be within calling distance of her mistress. A chamber pot was by the window, and a wash bowl was by the hearth.

She called to Fern, who instantly came out of the anteroom. Elaisse was glad to see her, for despite William's disdain of the working class, Elaisse liked Fern greatly and could never be stern with her. As a result, Fern was fiercely loyal to Elaisse. It was this loyalty that Elaisse counted upon for what she had planned that evening.

"I want to go out to the stable to see John tonight," Elaisse told Fern. "Please don't let anybody into your room. If my parents want to see me, tell them I'm asleep."

They waited until ten o'clock, then Elaisse opened her bedroom door. She peeked down the long hallways that were lighted by torches placed in holders on the stone walls. The torches shone, wavering from the drafts that gently blew down the corridors. The flickering flames created an illusion of shadow-creatures creeping stealthily through the passageways. She could hear her heart pound in her ears as she crept from her bedroom and hurriedly made her way down the hall.

She reached the main stairwell, desperately hoping that she would not be observed as she went down to the second floor of the keep where the exit was located. She wore slippers so that her tread would be silent, and she gathered her cloak and her simple tunic tightly around her to guard against the cold. Finally she reached the main entrance. A guard let her pass, having already been forewarned by Fern of Elaisse's passage and sworn to secrecy.

The night air was cool and crisp, and the sky was incredibly clear. The moon was a tiny crescent, so Elaisse felt secure that she would not be seen. Millions of stars shimmered and sparkled, and the night sounds were beautiful as frogs called and the last of the late season crickets sang. She took a deep breath of the fragrant night air, and felt how wonderful it was to be young and alive, with a future so full of promise if only she could marry the one she chose.

She made her way down the steps to the ground, then scampered along the castle grounds, holding her cloak tightly to hide her face. Her slippers had thin soles, and she felt every small pebble she stepped upon. She quickly navigated the castle road that led to the stable. She entered, and her nose was assaulted by scents of sweating animals and manure.

She stood there, watching, afraid; then a form came out of the darkness. John Wythe approached her and enveloped her in his arms.

Gripping her tightly, he whispered, "Tonight will be the night."

They kissed passionately, and then John took her hand and led her to a pile of clean, unused animal bedding. They kissed while he gently lowered her to the fragrant straw.

And then Elaisse panicked. She broke out of his embrace. "I can't do this," she said, trying to catch her breath. "I cannot behave as though I were a wife."

John drew back, and she could see his scowl even in the dim light of the stables. She knew his temper was short because his need was great. "I can't make you my wife unless you persuade your father to accept me as a son-in-law. If we do this thing I am asking, your father will either kill me or allow me to marry you. I'll take that chance."

"I can't," she said. "I shouldn't have come here; I see that now." She started to get up, but John pulled her back down upon the straw.

"I'm leaving tomorrow," he said.

"What! Leaving? Where? Why?"

"I've been ordered to France because their King Phillip is hostile. Our King Edward III has been patient, but now England must defend our territory in Normandy. Our past few months of peace are coming to an end. So you see, Elaisse, this is our last night together. You *must* give in to me."

When she started to object again, John kissed her on the mouth, stopping her protests. Gently but firmly, he pushed her backwards on the straw until she lay prone. He removed the cloak away from her head, and removed the strings that held her braids in place. Elaisse's long hair tumbled down and fell freely onto the straw, blending the similar colors of the fragrant bedding and her golden hair together. John combed his fingers through her hair, loosening the braids further. He seemed to delight as pieces of straw caught the golden strands and intertwined among them.

Then things continued from there. John pulled her tunic down over a shoulder, and she felt him taste her smooth skin with a flick of his tongue. He pressed her body down firmly into the straw so that she was unable to move away from him.

Her brain became inundated with confused thoughts as she fought feelings of panic. Half of her wanted John to continue, but the other, more dominant half had been conditioned by the rules of society. Virginity was a commodity that was highly valued, and if she lost it she could be ruined.

She had to decide. She had to decide *right now*, before it became too late. What should she do?

Should she let John continue to make advances upon her? Or stop the passion before it was too late? *Decide, decide!*

He began unwinding the cordage that was laced at her waist. That meant he was opening the front of her dress. He murmured softly, "If you can convince your father to allow our marriage, my title will be equal to yours."

What did he say? More importantly, what had he meant?

Elaisse felt anger at his words. Suddenly her decision was made. She pushed John off and sat up, pulling her dress closed around her. She could sense his confusion. But for her, the spell was broken.

"Why did you stop me?" John asked, his voice thick with impatience. "Did I hurt you?"

She looked directly into his face. "Do you love me? Or do you just want to take the title our marriage would give to you?"

"What!"

"I think my questions were clear."

"You sure know how to extinguish a man's desire," John said.

She re-laced her bodice. She was thinking that he hadn't answered her questions.

She knew he was angry and frustrated because he would have to remain unsatisfied on this night, but she was upset as well. She began to wind up her hair to tuck it under her cloak, and then

John stopped her.

He took a small knife from his shirt, and gently cut off a small lock of her hair.

"I'll keep this," he told her, "so that you will always be with me." He put the hair up to his nose. "It smells like the straw where we lay, and it looks like a ray of the sun. I'll keep it in a pocket next to my heart."

Was that the answer to her questions? Elaisse hugged him. "I don't think I am ready for what almost happened tonight. But maybe when you come back...when can you come back from France?"

"When I can," he said, "and that's all I know. But I will be back. And when I do, we'll finish what we started tonight. In the meantime, keep trying to change your father's mind about allowing me to marry you."

John kissed her a final time. Then she went out the stable door into the cool night and hurried back to her room in Wynham Castle.

Chapter Two

It was a ghost ship.

When the men from the dock climbed aboard, they cautiously walked along the deck and the galley. Unmindful of the creaking timbers, the five men banded together in an apprehensive group as they explored the upper level of the seemingly empty ship.

The men who were upon the drifting ship had been ordered to investigate the apparent abandonment of a seaworthy vessel. They took notice of the empty crow's nest, the deserted helm, and the vacant galley. Something was very wrong, indeed.

As a group, the men descended the companionway into the crew's quarters, which ran the width of the ship. They kept their heads down to avoid the low beams of the ship's bowels. The man nearest the front of the group tentatively reached to open a cabin door.

Inside the gloomy cabin, cockroaches scurried and rats scampered into the corners to hide in the darkness. The stench of rotting flesh and fetid feces bombarded the men's senses with overpowering intensity. Even before they saw the bodies, the five sailors instinctively knew that there were a lot of dead people on this particular ship.

Afraid to look, one man made the sign of the cross on his chest. But finally unable to resist, he too decided that he wanted to see the devastation. Together the five men gazed in alarm at what lay before their eyes. Collectively they had all seen horrible things, but nothing could have prepared them for what they witnessed now.

And as they stood paralyzed with horror, the five men completely ignored the rats that crept upside to the deck of the ship.

October 1348

Elaisse walked around as though in a daze; she went through the motions of everyday life but she knew that part of her soul was traveling on horseback in Normandy. Not a moment went by that she didn't think of John Wythe, and she prayed for his safety. In the presence of her parents, she pretended that nothing had changed. It was only to Fern that she could confide her longings and also her fears. Fern, who was only two years older than Elaisse, had a sympathetic ear and sealed lips.

But even to Fern, she could not express the concern that nagged at the corners of her mind, because the single sentence uttered by John on their last night together invaded her thoughts. Sometimes when she lay in bed late at night, she would picture him as he said, *If you can convince your father to allow our marriage, my title will be equal to yours.*

She analyzed that sentence over and over again in her mind. Most of the time she could dismiss the sentence as unimportant, but at other times, she couldn't help but to wonder at its significance. Did John love her? Really love her? She remembered that John had often told her *I want you*, but had he ever told her *I love you*?

And as the days melded into weeks, Elaisse once more became involved with her daily routines. She began to push John out of her mind because all the wondering about him went without answers. She realized that she would never have the answers to her questions until John came back from Normandy.

One Sunday morning, in early October, Fern and Elaisse dressed for church. They left the bedroom chamber and continued down the steep stone steps together, but parted on the second floor as they each walked to separate entrances of the castle's chapel. The chapel was located next to the great hall, and its ceilings were high. The chapel was separated into two seating arrangements. The household servants sat on stone pews on the floor and the privileged sat in the balcony. The clergy preached from the altar, known as a chancel, which was positioned at the front of the room.

On this cool October morning, Bishop Prenton welcomed his flock, then began his praises of the Almighty. He shifted to the subject of penance, and his thunderous voice filled the room as he began outlining reasons why the Lord was becoming increasingly intolerant of the sins of mankind.

"The failed crops are warnings from the Almighty," Bishop Prenton shouted at them with his booming voice. "People are selfish; they live only to seek the sins of the flesh. They lie and blaspheme. We need to get on our knees to beg the Almighty God to forgive us! We must repent from our sins! The great Lord God will no longer look past our transgressions!"

He paused for effect, then continued in a deadly calm voice, "And now there is word of a great pestilence coming out of France."

Elaisse gasped, and next to her, William shifted in his seat. The Lady Hildred gave no indication that she was listening.

Bishop Prenton told them, "In Avignon, rumors abound that masses of the population are beset with tumors in the groin and armpits. In Normandy, it is said that people are erect and healthy one minute, then falling to their deaths on the ground in the very next minute. In Burgundy, tales are told of mass graves that are filled to overflowing with countless dead. And in the Medical Facility in Paris, Pope Clement IV has requested that the doctors prepare reports on ways to reduce the spread of this great pestilence."

Again Bishop Prenton paused for effect. Then he thundered, "But still it spreads!"

The chapel was incredibly still, waiting for their leader in the faith to continue. Not a sound was heard; it was as though no one dared to move.

Elaisse silently told herself that England was shielded. Hadn't her father always said that God favored England? She calmed herself with the idea that the Bishop would never allow the sins of the French people to travel across the channel.

She thought, *England is good. Therefore, England is safe.*

But when Bishop Prenton began to speak again, his words were shocking. "There have been reported cases of this fearsome pestilence in Dorset. That is south of here, on the mother soil of England!"

All around Elaisse, pandemonium erupted in the congregation. Cries of fear and shouts of denial flowed from both the pews on the ground and in the balcony.

"Listen to me!" shouted the Bishop, and the people settled back into their seats, trembling, but quiet once again. "We must beg the Lord's forgiveness. Each of you! Beg the Lord immediately! Get down on your knees right now and pray with me for your own salvation, and for the salvation of England!"

The entire congregation immediately dropped to its knees, Elaisse included. Bishop Prenton bellowed a prayer at the top of his voice, beseeching God to have mercy and to forgive his faithful flock. She could hear the people praying reverently, some moaning softly and others brought to tears. Fear seemed to be the prevailing emotion, for if the rumors of this terrible pestilence were true, then it was a hideous affliction to be sure.

And now Elaisse wondered, *Could this peril really be invading English soil? Could it reach Suffolk, even Wynham Castle? Could the terrible fantasy stories of such a dreadful pestilence told by travelers possibly be true?*

And then she thought about John Wythe. He was in France where it was rumored that this ghastly illness was rampant. Was he safe? Or was John lying somewhere on the cold, wet, foreign ground, with no breath passing through his still lips?

She was brought back to the present when Bishop Prenton ended the service. People began leaving, dazed, as they vacantly stared ahead, seemingly numbed with shock.

But as soon as they left the chapel, people began noticing how normal their surroundings still appeared. Nothing seemed

29

changed. The sun still shone and the breezes still rustled the branches of the trees. No one appeared sick. Back in the environment of everyday life, nothing they had heard just moments ago seemed to be based on reality.

Elaisse felt the same way as the others. Once away from his booming, frightening voice, she thought, *Bishop Prenton may be a man of God, but he's still a man. And men have been known to be wrong.*

She looked at the departing congregation. She could hear snatches of conversation here and there as both the privileged and underprivileged left the chapel: *Aren't we good and faithful to our great and forgiving God? Don't we pray every night and go to chapel every Sunday? Aren't we already giving a great penance by living with such unusually high rainfall levels, cold climate, and widespread crop failures? Surely the good and righteous people of England are in God's favor!*

And so Elaisse, just like everyone else, consoled herself with denials. She pitied poor Dorset, but she told herself that Dorset was a seaport, full of sailors. And sailors were known to be blasphemers.

Within an hour after Bishop Prenton had broken the news of the pestilence reaching Dorset, Elaisse had convinced herself that any pestilence would be limited to a few sailors in that town. She could not fathom that the sickness could come to Wynham, so she told herself that it wouldn't. If she didn't believe it, then it couldn't be true.

And so after church, she went to the formal hall to dine with her parents. The dining hall's floors were strewn with rushes and straw to camouflage the dirt, and she stepped carefully over them. Bouquets of herbs and nosegays of flowers were strategically placed around the room to disguise any undesirable scents, and the sight of the indoor flowers cheered her.

She was affirmed in her denials when, at dinner, her father instructed her to ignore the Bishop's warning and to go on with her day without fear. At the table, William made it clear that his family was not to be troubled with Bishop Prenton's dire sermons.

"I think Bishop Prenton is concerned for the congregation, and that's very commendable," William said. "But clearly no one here is sick. The Bishop is a good man; a righteous man. Still, in this instance, I believe his concern for the people has exceeded the limits of reality. Bishop Prenton is overworked, and it is starting to show. Now, Elaisse, don't be troubled about it. I don't think we should waste our time worrying about something that has no chance of happening anywhere near Suffolk County, much less here at the castle."

William then changed the subject to what appeared to be his favorite topic, the on-going war with France. "England's army has a fantastic offensive position, with a united command center," he told his wife Hildred. "Now that our army has the new crossbow weapon, how much longer can King Phillip posture against England? His men are cowards; they run like rabbits!"

Elaisse broke in. "Have you heard any word of John Wythe?"

As a maid served the meal, William turned to Elaisse and said, "You should be thinking about Sir Geoffrey. I've spoken to him. He agrees to the unification of our families. The marriage is to take place next month, on Saint Martin's Day. November is blood month when we slaughter the animals to be preserved by the cold, so there will be plenty of fresh meat for the wedding feast."

Elaisse froze in her seat, shocked that the wedding was really going to happen. Her face drained of color. Jerking herself into motion, she cried out, "I won't marry Geoffrey!"

In contrast to Elaisse's white face, William turned very red. "Don't make a scene in front of the servants," he said through clenched teeth with a forced calm. "You are going to obey me. You *will* marry Geoffrey. After all, Elaisse, you are but a child, complete with a child's fantasies of what life is like. But I'm the adult. As your father and protector, I will make decisions for you."

"Wait—" Elaisse tried to interrupt.

William continued without letting her speak. "And if you

have any ideas about John Wythe, then you can just forget those ideas. John Wythe is dead, struck down in France!"

Elaisse sat still for another moment. Then, with a strangled cry, she jumped up from her seat and fled from the room.

She ran to her bedroom, and pounded on the maid's anteroom door. When Fern came rushing out, alarmed by the loud pounding, Elaisse flung herself on her bed and sobbed uncontrollably into her pillow. Fern became frightened for her mistress, and sat on the bed to try to soothe her. Fern coaxed Elaisse into sitting up on the bed and she held her in her arms. Fern let her cry without saying a word.

Elaisse began to talk through her grief. "It used to be that bad things could happen in the world, but I was here in Wynham Castle, so nothing ever affected me. Now I feel that my sanctuary is a lie because I realize the world outside this castle is very real, and it can touch me."

"What happened?" Fern asked.

"Oh my God in Heaven, John Wythe is dead, killed in France!" Elaisse wailed.

"I'm so sorry," Fern said, helpless to do or say anything else.

"My heart is sealed," Elaisse said. "The death of John has closed my heart. I never want to fall in love again."

And so she stayed in bed for two days, crying into her pillow, her heart broken by the death of the man who had once come so close to becoming her lover. In Elaisse's mind, the days were long but the nights were endless. Over and over again in her thoughts, she replayed that night with John in the stable that would now prove to be their last. If she had known at that time what she knew today, would she have given into his desires? Should she have consented, giving John a final gift that he would have taken to his grave? But what would that have done to her own life?

Finally she rose weakly from the bed where she had been emotionally imprisoned, and dressed to leave her bedroom for the first time in days.

William was delighted to see his daughter at the main meal

that day, always served at noon. "Elaisse, I'm glad to see you're feeling better. You've recovered just in time for the Harvest Home celebration tomorrow."

"Who is plowing the fallow field this year?" asked Hildred.

Elaisse was puzzled for a moment as she wondered what her mother was talking about. Then she remembered that for Harvest Home, a field that had been left to grow wild with weeds would be the site of a plowing race between four farmers, who would use their finest oxen to see who could plow the fastest, and who could produce the straightest rows. The villagers would select the four farmers, each chosen because of their strength and stamina.

"One of the chosen is Richard the Powerful, and he's my personal favorite," William answered his wife. He always delighted in any ceremony that contained contests and conquests.

"I'm looking forward to finding out who is going to be this year's Grape Maiden," Hildred said. The vineyards were to be picked at this time of year, and traditionally a young woman whom the men of the village voted to be the most beautiful would pick the first handful of grapes.

"Well now, Wife," William observed, "you must be in a very good mood today. Usually you don't say a word."

Hildred shrugged in response, and ate the rest of the meal in silence. Elaisse knew that her mother was conditioned, as were all ladies, to let the men take the lead on all matters of consequence. And on this day, Elaisse finished her meal just as silently as her mother.

The next morning, the sun was shining in an almost magical manner as it burned off the mist that floated upon the land. Elaisse and her family stepped back into the carriage for the short, bumpy ride to the village fields that lay just outside the castle walls.

All the people from Wynham Castle and the surrounding village gathered in the fields for the Harvest Home celebrations. Elaisse knew that this one would be grander than any previous Harvest Home festival that she had ever experienced. It was as though the villagers were trying to trick fate, by pretending that the dismal harvest yield was instead one of their most bountiful. Perhaps the villagers were determined to show God that if they could be thankful for this season's grim crop production, then perhaps He would take pity upon them and show mercy for the next season's weather.

And although Elaisse was supposed to stay close to her family, she sneaked off to wander through the festivities freely because she didn't want to miss a thing. The frolics began with minstrels singing gaily while colorfully dressed peasants strummed lutes and blew into wind instruments. A group of mummers then took the lead and spoke poetry without musical accompaniment. Finally, a troupe of actors, all adorned in harlequin dress, performed a play to the delight of the crowd.

The singing and the plays led up to the next activity. A pretty maiden from the village was pushed to the front of the crowd for the symbolic picking of the grapes. She was fourteen and had long, reddish-blonde hair that streamed freely from her ribboned head wimple. As she was pushed through, she was handed from person to person, and the spectators reached to touch her for the luck that legend promised she'd bring.

But the main event was the plowing contest. The four villagers chosen for the contest were all muscled, strong men, brown from long days of laboring in the sun. They laughed and joked as they taunted each other. For the benefit of the crowd, all four men loudly exclaimed how they would leave the other three in the dust. The crowd cheered and shouted encouragement as the four contestants shackled their oxen and readied their plows. The men were aligned in a row, ready for the starter to give them the signal.

Elaisse watched as the starter blew the horn and the contest began. The oxen surged forward, sweat already foaming on their flanks, the animals agitated from the noise of the crowd. The men attempted to keep their oxen in as straight a path as possible, crying "Ho!" and "Gee!" to guide them. The sharp plow blades tore through the earth as clods of dirt parted and fell by the wayside. The crowd ran alongside the plows, cheering and gesturing, causing the oxen to snort anxiously.

Suddenly it was neck and neck, the contest now between only two men as the others fell far behind. Richard the Powerful and Bertram the Brazen called to their oxen in unison. They gripped their plows firmly, because if the contest ended as a tie for speed, then the quality of the rows would be the determining factor to decide the victor.

Both men had sweat streaming down their faces from their efforts. They grunted with exertion. Their neck muscles stood out like cords and their arm muscles bulged from the demand placed upon them. The oxen seemed to react to the tension in the air; they pulled and strained to move quickly ahead.

One of the animals began to falter. It seemed lame in one leg. Bertram the Brazen screamed at this animal to go forward, to continue on! He seemed furious as his ox slowed and began to limp. Elaisse was caught up in the excitement as the crowd shouted jeers at Bertram, and she found herself joining in as they mocked him. With obvious anger, Bertram the Brazen halted his plow.

Richard the Powerful burst ahead, and all around her, the crowd went wild. Richard crossed the finish line, his ox snorting and panting. The crowd gathered around him, slapping his back, and someone handed him a large mug of ale.

Harvest Home came but once a year, a respite from the toils of back-breaking daily labor, and she could see that the peasants made the most of it. Wine and beer flowed freely, and musicians played cheerful songs. Men grew loud as they grew drunk, boasting to other men and courting the women with exaggerated chivalry.

Elaisse strolled away from the crowd to see the animals. The animals mooed or bleated as they were confined with tethers, displayed for sale or for trade to the crowd. The animals were exhibited as potential breeding stock, and she knew this day would be their last chance for respite. If the animals didn't find new owners here at Harvest Home, they would surely be slaughtered on Saint Martin's day. She knew that it made sense to kill the animals when the weather turned cold enough to keep the meat fresh for a longer stretch of time. Plus she knew it would save the precious grain for the breeding stock instead of wasting it on an excessive number of animal mouths to feed.

The day was long, and when it was finally over, Elaisse was tired. She was glad that her mourning for John was finished, and now she was eager to get on with a normal life.

She had no way of knowing that soon there would be nothing normal about her life at all.

Chapter Three

The rat felt hot.

Detecting a subtle change in the movement of the floor, the rat ventured carefully from its dark hiding spot, sniffing the air and peering cautiously as it crawled between two bales of cloth. The rat could not seem to comprehend the signals from its meager brain and so its movements were slow and its actions confused.

The rat suffered pains and had to stop moving from time to time to allow frequent spells of dizziness to pass. Sensitive to the moonlight, the rat hesitated at the doorway that led to the upper level, but then made the decision to proceed. Shudders rippled through its eight inch long black body as the rat ventured into the open air for the first time in months.

If anyone were to see this rat, it would be very obvious that the animal was sick. This rat had spreading boils on its underside, and in its bloodstream coursed *Yersinia pestis*. But no attempts were made to prevent the rat from making its escape.

The black rat was of a breed called *Rattus rattus* and they were common stowaways on ships. Its long, muscled tail helped maintain its balance as it ran from the bowels of the ship onto the open deck. Its dense fur, normally shiny and sleek, now appeared dull and lifeless in the moonlight. The rat's fevered brain instinctively guided the creature to search for fresh water in the hopes that its unquenchable thirst could be sated, and its internal heat could be cooled.

It sneaked, undetected, to a long, thick rope that moored the ship to the dock. The rat began climbing off the ship onto the shore that was England.

Early November 1348

"I'm going to run away," Elaisse confided to Fern. "Can you help me?"

"What do you want me to do?"

"You have relatives outside Wynham Castle," Elaisse said. "Will any of them take me in for a while?"

The two young women were strolling on the grassy meadow in front of the castle. They walked by the banks of a stream that bordered the castle wall. On the other side of the wall was the forest where the villagers gathered nuts, berries, and herbs. Often the villagers allowed their pigs to forage between the trees. But today, the forest was quiet, as the villagers were busy planting the fields with winter crops. Elaisse and Fern were undisturbed as they formulated the plans for Elaisse's secret departure.

Their feet crunched on dry leaves which had long ago fallen from the oaks on the other side of the castle wall. They formed a carpet of color. Somewhere there was a cook fire burning, and Elaisse could smell the familiar scent of smoke. She heard the calling of geese, and looked up to see the birds flying overhead in their "V" formation as they traveled on their southern journey. Her eyes misted, for Wynham Castle had been the only home she had ever known, and she expected to miss this lovely place. Already she was homesick, and she hadn't even left yet.

"A royal lady can't leave," Fern said.

"This royal lady can. But only if you help me."

"Are you sure this is what you want to do?"

"It's what I need to do."

"Well then, I have an uncle outside of Suffolk County, but he lives in London," Fern said. "I don't think London would be the sort of place you'd wish to go."

"Why not?"

"Well," Fern said, "I don't know how safe London is for a

finely bred woman like yourself. You couldn't let anyone know who you are, or you might be kidnapped and held for ransom. What I'm saying is that London has thousands of people, all living close together, and not every one of them is pleasant."

"I don't care!" Elaisse cried vehemently and stopped walking. "I won't marry Sir Geoffrey Gladden. I won't! I'd rather take my chances in a den of thieves."

"Den of thieves!" Fern laughed. "Well, I don't think it's *that* bad. As with anywhere people live, London also has its share of good people too. My uncle is one of them. His name is Taylor, Thomas Taylor. That's what he does."

They started walking again. "What do you mean when you say that's what he does?" Elaisse asked.

Fern laughed again. "I forget that you are in an upper class, and that you've never really been outside the castle walls. I consider you more of a friend than a mistress."

Elaisse thought to herself, *If my father heard Fern say that, he would have her beaten. That's just one of the ways my father and I are so different.*

"You still haven't told me what you mean," Elaisse reminded Fern.

"I mean that a lot of the people outside of nobility have last names that reflect their profession," Fern said. "For example, Smith stands for blacksmith. Then there are names such as Farmer, Miller, Potter, Baker, Mason, Gardener; the list goes on and on. My uncle's name is Taylor—he sews clothes. So did his father, and probably his grandfather as well."

"I never knew that," Elaisse said. "I only know people with last names such as Gladden, Prenton, Rothschild, and of course my own last name, Sheffield."

"Well," Fern said, "if you choose to go to London, you had better pick a much simpler name."

"I can't decide. Who shall I be?"

"If you didn't live in a castle, what sort of job would you prefer to do? Outside the castle, you'd have to have a job, you know."

"I have no idea." Elaisse realized it was true—she really didn't know what went on over the castle wall and she was very surprised at the thought. Her role in life was supposed to be to make a good marriage. "All I know is what I saw at Harvest Home. I certainly wouldn't want to be a Fisher or a Skinner. How about Hunter? What do you think of that name?"

"No," Fern disagreed. "Hunters are usually falconers who have some connection with castles. Why don't you pick something in the garment industry? That way, if you ask to be my uncle's apprentice, he may be more willing to accept you, if he thinks that dressmaking or some other type of garment making is in your blood."

"But his name is already Taylor. What does that leave for me?"

"How about Weaver?" Fern suggested. "That way people will think your family weaves wool into clothes and blankets. But you need to change your first name as well."

"How would I know that someone is talking to me if they don't call me Elaisse?"

"Pick something close to your real name."

"How about Elizabeth?"

Fern smiled. "Elizabeth it is. I'll send a messenger to my uncle that a villager named Elizabeth Weaver will be coming to request an apprenticeship. Of course, he'll expect payment, and you could pay up to six pounds. The garment guild allows masters of apprentices to charge between two pounds for the minimum and six pounds for the maximum. So you should come prepared, because it will be my uncle's decision about the fee. You are lucky that his last apprentice died, so he doesn't have any now. Well, the apprentice wasn't lucky, of course."

"Is the work hard enough to kill someone?" Elaisse asked.

"Of course not. That's not why the apprentice died," Fern said. "But living in London is harder on everyone than it is here. Elaisse, are you sure you want to do this? Why would you want to trade this good life for the hard life of a laborer? Have you thought this through?"

40

Elaisse thrust out her chin in defiance. "If I married Sir Geoffrey, my life would be over before it even had a chance to begin. There is a whole world out there and I've experienced none of it. I won't marry Sir Geoffrey at any cost."

"The cost could be high indeed," Fern said, "and I am not talking about the apprenticeship fee."

"London cannot possibly be that bad. You said that good people like Thomas Taylor live there."

"But what if you wind up being a dressmaker all your life? What if fate decides you are never to come back to Wynham Castle?"

"By the time the oak leaves have grown green with life again next summer, I'll be back," Elaisse said. "I just want to give Geoffrey Gladden enough time to find another wife. My father cannot permanently expel me from Wynham Castle. It is my birthright to be here. Besides, Daddy loves me."

"If you're sure," Fern said, the doubt sounding in her voice. "When do you want to leave?"

"Tonight."

"So soon?" Fern sounded sad. Then she became all business. "There's a messenger going to London in about an hour. The messenger is taking Sir William's business, but I know him, and he'll take my message for five or six shillings. I'll ask him to deliver the message to Uncle Thomas. And here in the castle, I'll tell the guard at the keep that you'll be going out tonight after dark. I just won't mention that you won't be back."

"But I will be back next summer," Elaisse said. "In the meantime, I'm probably going to miss you most of all."

"Miss me?" Fern asked. "I am but your maid."

"Oh, stop being so formal," Elaisse said, and the two women hugged.

When they separated, Fern said, "One more thing. You are going to need an escort to London."

"Why?"

"No proper lady travels alone. That's just not done, and for good reason; it's not safe. Besides, how would you find your way? You'll need an escort who has traveled to London many times, so you won't get lost. Or robbed. Or worse!"

Elaisse didn't like the sound of that. "What do you mean by worse?"

"Never mind," Fern said quickly. "I know who to ask to guide you. I'll send him to the east entrance of the wall tonight at ten. He'll have a horse for you."

"You think of everything! And I thank the Lord God that you do."

"Well, it will also cost you for the horse."

"I don't care. I have plenty of money. I can take all I want out of my father's treasury. He won't find out until after I'm gone."

And so it was settled.

That afternoon, Elaisse packed a small satchel. The intention was for her to travel light, taking gold coins instead of clothes. She anticipated that, working for a dressmaker, she would be making her own clothes once she arrived in London. Plus, food and shelter would be provided if Thomas Taylor agreed to take her on as an apprentice. But if Master Taylor refused, then the coins would help her find another direction to take. She had learned that there were no problems for those who had money; it made life easy. She figured that London would be easy as well.

The preparations for the departure had an unreal quality, and Elaisse felt as though she was acting out one of the plays she had seen during Harvest Home. It was as though she was looking as someone else's behavior through her own eyes. When the time to leave neared, she began having second thoughts as she wondered, *How could I really be planning such a drastic change in my life? I've never even peeked beyond the castle walls before! How do I know what is out there?*

But Elaisse calmed herself with the thoughts that she had no other choice. Her father wanted her to marry Sir Geoffrey in five days. All in the castle were preparing for the Saint Martin's day wedding and the accompanying feast. But she wanted to follow her heart, and she told herself she would be willing to sacrifice everything she had ever known in order to do so.

Darkness enveloped the castle grounds, and the clock approached ten. Elaisse knew it was time to go. She was warmly dressed and made sure she wore firm, pointed-toe shoes that had low heels and sturdy soles. She hugged Fern a final time. Picking up the satchel made of cloth, Elaisse cracked open her wooden bedroom door to take a peek into the hallway.

Nobody was in sight.

The passageway was cold, lit by the torches on the walls but not warmed by them. The torches released their smoke into the hall, causing the walls to be covered with a fine layer of soot.

Elaisse could smell the sweet fennel, rosemary, and lavender that were strewn with the rushes and straw on the floor. She could also smell the faint underlying foulness of grease, body odor, and chamber pots that permeated most of the castle.

Clutching her satchel and pulling her coat tightly around her, she ventured into the passageway. She welcomed the dimness of the hall to help camouflage her escape, but in some places, the passageway was very black. She was afraid because her imagination created all sorts of vile images as to what could be lurking in the dark corners.

She reached the main stairwell. She felt the pounding of her heart as the fear gripped her tightly. She was desperately hoping that she would not be observed as she went down to the second floor of the keep where the exit was located. Elaisse was thinking that she had never been caught while sneaking out of the castle at night for her meetings with John Wythe—would this be the night that her luck wore out?

She passed the guard who stood propped against the wall at the entrance to the keep. He didn't acknowledge her, and Elaisse didn't know if it was because he was paid by Fern for his silence or if he was asleep.

Hastening down the stairs, she was aware that the steps were wet and slippery. She thought, *Wouldn't it be ironic if I fell and broke my neck, dying before I even had a chance to get to London where the real danger is supposed to be?*

But she made it to the bottom safely, and continued quickly

across the castle towards the lawn outside.

She hurried across the meadow. Dewy grass sparkled in the moon's glow, and again the beauty of Wynham Castle struck her. The air was damp but smelled sweet, and the night was quiet except for a late-season screech owl that shrilled as it hunted rodents in the darkness. Right before she reached the east wall of the castle grounds, she paused and turned around for a final look at Wynham Castle, which had been the only home she had ever known.

I won't cry, she thought. *From now on, I will be a much stronger person than I have ever been before.*

She reached the castle wall. The guard there did not speak, but nodded his head slightly to her as he opened the gate. She knew that he had been paid well for this secret service, but if he were caught in the act of allowing her escape, he would be imprisoned, or worse, hanged. She was grateful that his greed overcame the adversity to risk.

Again, Elaisse was convinced that as long as she had money, all would be right. Didn't money give her control over everything in the world? Of course it did.

The gate closed behind her. Now she was on the other side, outside in the world. She stood uncertainly. A new fear gripped her. What if no one was here to meet her? What if the escort decided not to show? What would she do then?

The moon's reflection allowed some visibility as Elaisse took a step forward. She wondered, *Should I call out? Or should I search in silence for my escort? Or should I face the idea that he didn't show up, and go back to the castle to try again another night?*

Then she heard a horse snort and jangle its bridle. A man appeared from behind a bush, riding a horse and leading another. The riderless horse was very large, dark brown, and seemed spirited.

Elaisse was inwardly overjoyed to see that her escort had come. Suddenly her knees felt weak. She had not realized she had been holding her breath before the man's arrival and now she let the air out in a rush.

As she mounted the large brown horse, she thought, *This is really happening! There's no turning back now. I'm on my way to London. I'm on my way to an adventure!*

Chapter Four

The rat was in its death throes.

Its nest was one of many nests in the thatched roof of a cottage, hidden among the straw, rushes, and sod used as roofing material. Under normal circumstances, the cottage roof would have provided ideal conditions for rats to live and multiply, as the thatch could easily be gnawed, and tunnels would go unnoticed by humans. Under normal circumstances, the darkness of nightfall would have provided excellent cover for rats to venture into the living quarters of humans and thereby steal food.

But this rat would never gnaw tunnels or steal food ever again. They dying animal shuddered as it gasped for breath. Blindly snapping at the air, it experienced progressive paralysis until one by one, its internal organs began to shut down.

Suddenly it lay still.

From the rat's cooling body, desperate fleas emerged, sensing that their host was dead. Now the fleas, all infected with *Yersinia pestis*, found themselves in the roof of a peasant household. They deserted the lifeless rat in the quest for new hosts whose fresh blood could be consumed.

In the search for new hosts, some of the fleas fell from the ceiling straw down to the cottage floor below. Unable to seek out their preferred hosts, these fleas turned to the only warm bodies they could locate, which were the humans who were sleeping in their beds.

And gradually, a very deadly bacterium traveled northward from the tiny cottages of Dorset. *Yersinia pestis* was making its way towards the crowded living conditions of London.

Late November 1348

They rode in silence for about half an hour, and because Elaisse was unsure of what to say to this strange man who rode beside her, she said nothing. The darkness made getting a good look at him impossible, although in the moonlight she could tell that the man was tall and his hair was long. Finally she could stand it no longer, and asked him his name.

"Now," he said in a deep, melodic voice, "do you think it is in my best interests to give you my name? And if I asked yours, would you give me your real name, or a new one that you've just invented?"

"Don't you care who I am?" Elaisse asked, surprised at this man's apparent lack of curiosity.

"No, I don't care who you are. I've already been paid handsomely for this trip to London. That's all I care about."

They rode in silence for a minute while she digested that. Finally she asked, "Well then, what shall I call you?"

"You can call me Roger. And what do *you* want to be called?"

"I'm Elizabeth," she lied, trying her new identity on for size.

"If you say so."

They rode in the darkness for about three hours. Unused to riding long distances, Elaisse finally told Roger that she could not go on. It was about one in the morning, and she was not used to staying awake so long. The adrenaline that she had felt earlier in the evening had now been exhausted, and she was tired and feeling cross.

"I need to stop," she told Roger. "I need to sleep somewhere."

"I'll make a bed of grass, leaves, and blankets," Roger said. "We'll sleep until dawn, and then we'll need to be off again."

"What!" Elaisse cried. "Are you saying you want us to sleep outside? In this cold night air?"

Roger laughed, and she thought it was an inappropriate time for humor.

"I don't know where you think you are," he told her. "You

may have come out of Wynham Castle, but now you are out in the rest of the world. There are no cottages around in these parts, and even if there were, I was told to keep you hidden until we get to London. You'd better wise up. I know you're on the run, and you'd better start using your head or else you'll never get very far with your new life."

She bristled at his lecture. "Who do you think you are? What are you, some sort of criminal? A smuggler? A thief? You make money by doing illegal things, like taking runaways to London!"

Roger reined his horse to a stop. "Of course I make my money doing illegal things. Why do you think I am escorting you? It's certainly not because I like associating with the upper class."

Elaisse stopped her horse as well. She unleashed her temper. "You make upper class sound like a dirty word. I'll have you know that my parents are fine and decent people."

"Your parents use and abuse anyone who is under their station in life."

She felt her face grow hot. "My father takes good care of the villagers. Without nobility, the peasants would flounder. They'd have no direction, no leadership, and absolutely no protection from outlaws like yourself."

Roger burst into laughter, which only angered her further, and she shouted, "There's nothing funny!"

He quieted, then said in a grim voice, "Without nobility, the peasants might have something that resembles a real life. As it is right now, the peasants cannot stand up for themselves or else they'd be jailed. They are suppressed by force and threats of imprisonment. They have to pay outrageous rents or else they'd be jailed. They have to turn over most of their crops for which they toil so hard or else they'd be jailed."

"It's the law," Elaisse said. "The peasants must be held in their place or else there would be anarchy. My father knows this."

"You're talking a lot about your father," Roger said. "You'd better be more careful as to what you say to people. I'm paid not to tell anyone about you, even though yes, I know who you are. But the next time you talk about nobility, you might not get so lucky. You might run your mouth off to someone who could do you some harm. Some people aren't going to be agreeable to your opinions, especially the people who are hungry and overworked, so you'd better watch what you say."

"You'd better, you'd better!" Elaisse cried. "Is that all you know how to say?"

He paused, then continued, "Open your ears and listen when someone gives you good advice! Believe me, you are going to need your wits about you. You'll need to learn quickly out here in the world. It's to your own benefit to pay attention and to learn everything you can, and to make the most out of every opportunity. And for God's sake, stop talking about your father. It gives you away."

She calmed down. She knew he was right. She realized that she had a lot of changing to do, and not just her name.

Roger clucked to his horse, rode over to a small clearing underneath some trees, and dismounted. Elaisse followed him and also dismounted. He showed her how to gather the bedding material, and how to search out grasses and leaves that were dry as he passed over the foliage that was wet with dew. He made sure the horses were securely tied so they wouldn't wander in the night. Roger spread a blanket, and she gratefully lay down, pulling another blanket over her. It was scratchy but warm. She fell into a deep sleep almost immediately.

Morning came too quickly, and Roger shook her awake. Elaisse sat up, her golden hair tousled and entangled with leaves. She took a brush out of her satchel, and began combing out her hair and then wrapping it tightly into braids. The morning air smelled fresh and fragrant, and the earth emitted the musty, pungent scent of rotting leaves. She realized, with a surprise, how pleasant waking up to a crisp, crystal clear morning in the country could be.

Suddenly she became aware of Roger looking at her. She stopped braiding, and looked back at him. "What?"

Roger grinned, embarrassed at having been caught staring so blatantly. "Last night I didn't know how beautiful you are. Or so young. How old are you?"

"I'll be seventeen in three weeks," she said. She stared back at him. She was surprised to see that he was handsome, around twenty years old, and had long hair almost the same golden color as her own. His beard was not yet thick, giving away his youth.

He wore a heavy brown tunic and a woolen cloak that was gathered at his waist by a braided belt. His leggings, called chausses, were tied with strings to another belt under his tunic. His shoes were pointed as were all the style that year.

As she continued to stare, taking him in, Roger suddenly smiled at her, and she was amazed at how his features were transformed into someone who seemed friendly and kind. The smile created dimples in his cheeks and beneath his lips were straight, white teeth.

"Now who's looking at whom?" he grinned, playfully taunting her.

She blushed. "It's just that I'm surprised at your appearance. I expected you to be somebody more sinister, considering what you do for a living."

"You mean, considering that I am a 'criminal' who gets 'paid for taking runaways to London?' You're thinking that I might not be the monster you thought I should be?"

He was still grinning.

"I suppose that's right," she said, smiling back at him.

But then he stopped smiling, and his face hardened into granite. "Now you're taking things on face value without finding out what lies underneath. Here's something else you've got to learn. You'd better realize that you shouldn't judge people by the way they look. Bad people don't always look like ogres. They can look just like you or me."

She withdrew, her feelings hurt.

He stopped and his features softened. "I don't mean to keep lecturing you. But I've always considered persons of nobility to be 'the oppressors' and I was taking my anger out on you. I suppose it works both ways; now that I've met someone from the upper class, you've helped me to realize that persons of nobility may not always be bad people either."

She didn't want to be soothed by him. "I'm not ashamed of who I am. Besides, none of us chooses where to be born."

Roger got up and went to the horses, untying the reins. He re-filled the saddlebags in preparation to resume their trip, and said over his shoulder, "If you were so happy being who you were, then why are you running away from Wynham Castle?"

"Because my father had decided my future without considering my feelings, and I wanted some say in my own life," she burst out, then stopped herself. After all, hadn't he just been telling her to keep her own counsel?

He came back to sit beside her. "Just like the peasants should have some say in their lives as well."

"I don't want to talk about it!" Elaisse cried with exasperation. "Just stop."

They mounted their horses and resumed their trip in silence. After an hour, the silence became uncomfortable. Roger decided to speak, breaking the icy feel of the mood.

"You're right," he said, "let's talk of other things."

"Like what?"

"Well," Roger said, "you haven't seen much of the world, so I'll tell you about it. England has a lot of different terrain. In the Fens near Lincolnshire, there lies a vast marsh. South of Bristol, there's a high plateau that has moors and such. And by the Strait of Dover, there are hills made of chalk."

"No!" Elaisse laughed at how ridiculous it sounded. "Hills can't be made of chalk!"

"It's true," Roger said. "Plus, England has all sorts of different climates, depending upon where you are. Some parts have beautiful weather. But other places, like Pennine, have a lot of fog. London can get pretty cold in December and January. It can even snow there."

"Tell me more about London," she encouraged.

"London has more people in one city than you've probably

ever seen anywhere in your life," he said. "To control crime, most parts of London have curfews of either nine or ten o'clock at night. Taverns and shops close down at curfew, and people are supposed to go inside their houses, although some don't."

"London sounds exciting," she said, "but it also sounds a bit intimidating."

"There are over a hundred churches in London," Roger continued. "The biggest one is Saint Paul's Cathedral, located right in the middle of the city. I've heard that churches have problems with rats chewing on the hymnals."

"That's another tall tale!" Elaisse laughed. "Rats don't eat books."

"Maybe not eat them, but paper makes great nesting material. London has problems with rats and mice. There're a lot of them. That's partly because the people of London tend to throw their garbage out into the streets. That draws the rats. But the rats help get rid of the garbage that would otherwise simply rot, so it's not all bad. Plus, rats don't really bother people all that much. The rats and people live together."

"I think the rats would bother me," she said.

"No, you'll get used to rats," he told her. "In fact, there are a lot of things about London that you'll need to get used to. For example, the buildings are close together and very tall. They block out the sun, so a lot of streets are sort of dim. At first you'll feel like you're in a canyon, because it's different from where you used to live. In the country, cottages are low and spread out, so everything is sunny. But in London, most streets are always in the shadows."

"No!" Elaisse exclaimed.

"It's true."

After a while, the two riders became quiet and the journey turned into one of monotony. Elaisse felt that they were riding endlessly. She kept moving her hips to keep time with her horse's gait, but still, she was unused to hour after hour in the hard saddle. Lunch was altogether too brief, and Elaisse quickly found herself back in the saddle for more hours of travel. Finally the sky darkened as night began to arrive, and she told Roger that she wanted to stop riding for the day. Her fanny was sore, and she was so very, very tired.

"When will we reach London?" she asked irritably as she dismounted for the night. Her mood was dark.

"Probably tomorrow around late afternoon," Roger told her. He tethered the horses securely, and pulled dried jerky and fruit from his saddlebag. "Tomorrow night you'll probably get a real supper, but for tonight, we're going to have to eat the same sort of thing we had for lunch."

Once off her horse, Elaisse immediately felt better. After she and Roger had eaten, she helped him make up the bedding. She felt proud that she was learning how to do things for herself. The night was cold, and she snuggled under her blanket as Roger lay down a few feet away. Soon she could hear him breathing evenly, and she knew he was asleep.

The night was quiet, because the frogs and crickets had already begun their hibernation. A breeze rustled through the trees, causing leafless branches to groan and creak as they moved in the wind. It was very dark, for the moon was only a sliver in the sky, and random clouds drifted across the stars. She could smell the dampness of the earth, and was uncomfortable on the hard surface of the ground that wouldn't give when she shifted her weight.

Suddenly she thought she heard something different, something that caught her attention. It sounded like a night creature was moving through the underbrush. She strained her ears to hear.

Is it an animal? she wondered. Her next thoughts were, *Is it coming this way? Should I wake Roger?*

She continued to listen. For a moment, the night sounds were only the breezes softly blowing through the trees. But then, *there!*

She heard it again, a branch on the ground snapping under something's weight, and bushes being pushed aside. Something was coming, she was sure of it now. She could feel her heart race and heard the pounding of her own blood in her ears.

She knew she had to wake Roger. But she stayed under her blanket, as though the thin woolen material could protect her from whatever was coming. She trembled, knowing that whatever it was, she needed Roger's help. She thrust the blanket off of her face so she could yell to him.

Just as she started to open her mouth, a rough hand clamped over it and she felt something sharp at her throat. The cold metal against her skin felt like a knife, and a large one. She struggled, hopelessly entangled in her blanket. Someone was holding her down. She could smell his odor and feel his strength.

"Where's your money?" The stranger whispered hoarsely against her ear, and his breath was hot and stinking. "I'll take my hand away from your mouth so you can tell me. Don't scream or I'll slit your throat!"

"In my satchel," Elaisse gasped when the hand left her mouth.

Suddenly the man began violently shaking her. Then for no apparent reason, his hold loosened and she tumbled out of his grasp, landing abruptly on the hard ground.

She threw off the blanket that confined her. She rolled away as quickly as she could and then rose to flee. But the sudden, strange gargling noise that came from the stranger made her stop to turn around and look back.

It was Roger!

Roger had the man in his clutches. And Elaisse realized that was why the man had let her go, because Roger had grabbed him off of her.

She stood still, speechless and amazed. She watched as Roger dropped the man onto the ground. The stranger lay prone, his head at an odd angle and he no longer moved.

"He's dead," Roger said, panting from exertion. "I killed him with his own knife."

He paused, calmed his breathing, then turned towards Elaisse. "Are you all right?" he asked. "Did he hurt you?"

"No," she said, still trembling. "I'm just scared. Really scared."

Roger walked towards her to take her into his arms. "It's over now," he soothed.

She pushed him away. She began to realize the enormity of the situation. "We killed a man! That's a sin against God. What should we do?"

He reached for her but again she pushed him away.

"How dare you touch me!" she cried.

"What?" Roger appeared stunned at the change in her. Just a moment ago, she had seemed helpless and afraid.

Elaisse turned away from Roger and looked at the dead man on the ground. She felt overwhelmed with the enormity of it all. "The Lord God will surely punish us for killing this man. Maybe He'll strike us down with the pestilence that I've been hearing so much about."

Roger looked at her oddly. He was quiet for a moment as he continued to stare at her. Then he spoke, "It is no sin to kill in self-defense."

"Is that how you justify it before the eyes of God?"

"Yes," Roger said. "This man would certainly have killed you. Somebody had to be killed tonight. I just got to him first. And as for the pestilence, God has nothing to do with that."

Elaisse was astounded. "How can you say that? Bishop Prenton says the sickness is to punish the sinners in the world!"

"It's time you started thinking for yourself."

He walked back to the stranger lying on the ground, and lightly kicked him over to get a look at his face. He stood there silently, taking in what he saw of the dead man's face. Then he said, "I've seen this man before."

"You have?" Curiosity got the better of her and she came over to look at the dead man, his face staring with sightless eyes into his own private view of eternity.

"Yes," Roger said, "I'd seen him outside of Wynham Castle. Stupid of me. I should have known that we were being followed."

Elaisse gasped. "You mean he had planned to rob us all along?"

Roger grinned sardonically. "Well, well, Elizabeth. Meet your first bad guy. I'm sure you'll meet many more before your little adventure in London is finished."

"Little adventure! You're so awful!" Elaisse shouted, unnerved. "Yes, this is obviously not a person of the highest caliber. But not everybody in this world is evil! Like my father…he's a very good man…he means well…" she trailed off, suddenly very homesick.

She went back to her blanket and sat down. She was tired, upset, and bewildered. She put her head in her hands and rubbed her temples. She paid no attention when Roger moved the body of the stranger into the bushes, and didn't look when he covered the body with leaves and branches.

"Soon the animals will remove all traces of him," he told her when he returned.

"Did I really need to know that?" Elaisse spoke through her hands, which were still holding her head.

Roger came over and sat next to her. He didn't speak; he just sat and let her feel his nearness. After a while he put his left arm around her shoulders, seeming to test her reaction. When she didn't react at all, he pulled her closer to him with his left hand. He used his other hand to touch her hair, then he gently moved her hands away from her face. He touched under her chin and lifted her head. He tried to kiss her but she pushed him away.

"I can't," she said, her voice sounding strained and foreign to her own ears.

Roger sighed, and got up off the blanket.

"You don't have to leave," she told him.

He stopped, seeming to loom above her as he stood, so tall in the moonlight. "You've pushed me away."

Elaisse sat up straight and frowned. "My father would be horrified if he knew that you tried to kiss me. He'd send you to the gallows."

"Your father. Your father. Always your father." Roger sighed. "You think you have run away from your father, but in reality you're taking him right along with you, aren't you?"

"You don't need to talk to me like that."

"Like what? Want to know what I think? If you really wanted

to obey the rules of your father's house, then you never would have left in the first place. So let go of your father. Leave him behind where he belongs. Start thinking for yourself."

She was angry but realized that she was too tired to argue. Suddenly she was incredibly sleepy. The combination of the long trip, the stress of the stranger's attack and subsequent death, and the unexpected advances from Roger, all left her exhausted.

"The night's not over, so I would like to sleep some more," she told Roger. "Do you think we'll be safe?"

"I think we've already seen all the excitement we're going to see for one night," he assured her.

So Elaisse crawled into her blankets on the hard, cold ground. She was too tired to notice any discomfort any more, and quickly fell into a deep sleep.

The next morning she awoke before Roger, and considered her situation as she listened to him breathe softly and steadily over in his bedding of blankets. She was confused over her mixed emotions about someone as mysterious and contrary as Roger seemed to be. He was uncouth, hardened, and had killed a man effortlessly. Yet at other times, he could seem almost kind, and after all, he had saved her life.

She mentally reviewed the previous night's events, and she imagined once again the feel of the knife as it was held against her throat. She vividly recalled how slowly time had seemed to pass when Roger let the stranger simply drop to the ground after he had killed him. The robber had seemed to endlessly fall until he had landed in a heap upon the cold, hard earth.

It made her feel uneasy to recall the emotions that had passed through her mind at the time: a collection of horror, fear and—she hated to admit it—a thrill she had never experienced before. She was discovering things about herself that truly amazed her. And some of the things shocked and repulsed her.

She didn't know what she was becoming, but she felt she was changing just as caterpillars emerged from their safe cocoons to become different beings entirely. She was discovering emotions and ideas that had slumbered in a life of routine. Elaisse felt that she was emerging from the cocoon of childhood. What lay ahead?

A sound from Roger brought her back to the present. She gazed at him across the few feet of meadow that separated them and he grinned at her, any hardness absent from his face. Neither spoke or made any moves to get out of the blankets.

Instead, Roger turned to lie on his back, and, mimicking him, Elaisse did likewise. She listened to the winter birds awaken, and watched as the sun created prisms out of the early morning clouds. The clouds marched in formations across the sky, producing beams of light that streamed towards the ground as the sun peeked between them.

She breathed in the crisp, clean fall air. *I could stay out here for a long time,* she thought, *if only nightfall never came.*

Then Roger sat up and told her they needed to get back into the saddle. She felt dirty and grimy from sleeping on the ground. *Perhaps when I arrive in London,* she thought, *I'll risk a full bath.*

She knew that baths were dangerous to one's health. Baths opened the pores in the skin and allowed the flux to enter the body. Baths made the skin wrinkle, so that was proof that it could age a person before his or her time, doing terrible damage. These were the reasons why almost all of the people only washed the exposed parts of their bodies: the hands and face. Baths were reserved for times when the dirt and sweat became so unbearable that it was worth the risk of catching the flux and becoming permanently wrinkled.

Maybe if I keep the water temperature cool, she thought, *the bath won't make me old and sick. If I'm careful and do it quickly, I'll be spared the horrible impurities that baths can bring.*

Back on the horses, the day passed quickly. At around noon there was a slight drizzle. Although the rain didn't last long, the day continued to darken as the clouds thickened. Elaisse and Roger rode through one village after another, and they began to see more and more people on the trail.

Eventually the trail widened to become a road, and Elaisse

realized that soon she would experience London for the first time in her life.

They arrived at one of the seven gates on the outskirts of the city. The gate they chose was so large that it housed a prison inside. People were everywhere—Elaisse had never seen so many people. They were all milling about and each seemed to be rushing to complete some sort of urgent errand.

She saw that Roger had been right about the buildings; they towered over the streets and blocked the sunlight. The streets were narrow and dark, with houses overhanging everywhere. Some had flags flown in front to mark shops. Many shops appeared to have apartments on top, on the second or third floors. A good number of the buildings were decorated with signs containing paintings of lions, eagles, rams, and other animals.

Elaisse found the city both amazing and bewildering. London was certainly an awesome sight for a country visitor. She felt apprehensive, yet excited.

She and Roger guided their horses through the crowded streets. Children were everywhere; they ran and darted between horses and carts. Dogs and poultry were abundant, wandering around at will, and an occasional pig could be seen rooting in the dirty streets.

In London, it appeared as though all classes of people were intermingled, because regal people dressed in finery walked the same streets as people in rags.

But it was the stench in the air that Elaisse noticed most. A smell of rot predominated. She looked at her surroundings and saw that gutters from the roofs carried not only rainwater runoff, but also kitchen refuse that people unloaded into them. Filth that obviously had been dumped from chamber pots lay in open trenches alongside the roads.

Anything and everything that no longer had a use was simply discarded in the streets to be either picked up and reused by another, or to merely lie there until the elements or the rats disposed of it.

Elaisse felt a growing sense of dread as she viewed the filthy city. She wondered, *Is this to be my new home? Oh no, what have I done? Lord God, please give me strength!*

Roger continued to steer her through the crowded and dirty streets. Eventually they arrived at the address of Thomas Taylor, and Roger reined his horse to a stop. He helped Elaisse dismount, his touches lingering longer than necessary.

"Well, here you are!" Roger said.

She looked at him. "Will you ever be back?"

He grinned, and Elaisse found him handsome. "I shouldn't come back, but I probably will. If I did, would you want to see me?"

She hesitated, then ventured, "I think so."

"I'd like to see you again, too."

"When?"

"I don't know. I have some things to do first, and some people to meet. But eventually, I'll come back and find you. In the meantime, you need to get familiar with your new home, Elaisse."

She realized he had not called her Elizabeth. "You know who I am?"

He laughed. "I've known all along. I always make it my business to know everything about the risks I take in life."

"And so, who are you? Is your name really Roger?"

He was still smiling. "That's my first name. But my last name is nobody's business. Not even yours. My first name is all you will ever need to know. Now, let's go talk to Thomas Taylor."

But it turned out that Thomas Taylor had never gotten word that Elaisse was to arrive. He had never heard of her. Roger stepped in to negotiate an apprenticeship. It was true, Thomas admitted, that he was in need of an assistant. It was also true that payment would be appreciated.

"But," Thomas protested, "how old is she? Sixteen, you say? She is too old to be a beginning apprentice. New apprentices are only nine years old, ten at the most."

Elaisse jumped into the discussion. "My last name is Weaver," she lied. "It's true that I spent my youth as a maid in

60

the house of a lady. But because of my heritage, I will instinctively have a feel for secure stitching and accurate measurements."

She had no idea if she could live up to her promises, although she knew she would try her best. But Elaisse understood that she needed room and board, and Thomas could provide that for her. She smiled inwardly as she realized how Roger's lessons about surviving out in the world seemed to be taking hold.

Thomas scrutinized her closely, then said, "Because of your age, I will charge you the maximum that the garment's guild will allow. That's six pounds. Are you willing to pay that amount?"

Roger spoke. "The garment's guild also promises safety for the apprentice. She is not to be touched or molested in any way."

Thomas' face reddened with anger. "What you are suggesting is a sin! I am a God-fearing man, a gentleman of my word!"

"Of course you are," Elaisse soothed. "Forgive Roger; he is not always appropriate." *There,* she thought, *I finally got you back, Roger.*

Roger burst out laughing, and Thomas said to Elaisse, "He is unhinged as well, so I will talk directly to you. Are you willing to work very hard?"

She said yes and the deal was done.

Roger bade her farewell. As he was leaving, he winked at her.

Elaisse watched him ride away. She was surprised to realize that she felt a sense of loss when he was gone.

Chapter Five

The man emitted a stench of horrific foulness.

He lay on his bed of linen-covered straw and groaned, but he did not realize that he made any sound. The man was alone in his London tenement, for at the first sign of his illness, his family had fled, leaving him to fend for himself.

This he was not doing very well, because he was dying.

What began as small lumps in his armpits had evolved quickly into large buboes under both arms and in his groin. They were black with engorged blood and swelled to almost bursting. The buboes were growing to the size of eggs in his armpits, and to the size of an apple in his groin. Blood and pus oozed out of these hard, smooth growths, smelling fetid and causing excruciating pain for the victim.

If anyone were to witness this scene, they would observe that the man's body was spotted with dark blotches as internal bleeding ravaged his system. Fever caused intense sweating. Boils had spread over his face, arms, and chest, leaking rancid pus that no one was around to clean off of him. The man lapsed into a coma; a final, merciful blessing.

As the man died, his sphincter relaxed and blood-blackened excrement stained the bed. The tenement was so putrid that no one would live there again for a long, long time.

The terrible suffering and subsequent death would soon spread beyond this house. Unfortunately, when the man's family fled, they unknowingly took the fleas that had crawled into their clothes along with them.

December 1348

Elaisse found London overwhelming, bombarding her senses with excessive stimulation. Everything appeared to loom larger than life. There were more people in the few square miles of the city than she had ever imagined could be living in the entire world. It seemed as though everyone in the crowded city rushed around in a hurry, and Elaisse couldn't believe the different classes of people that walked side-by-side through the streets.

But still the difference between the poor and the rich were obvious. The rich lived together in better houses, and wore furs and had fine horses. Even though they strode the same streets as the poor, the rich turned up their noses and ignored anyone they felt was beneath them. In turn, the poor mocked the rich and made no attempts to disguise their scorn.

She had begun her apprenticeship under Thomas Taylor just a month ago, when he took her into his household. She had been relieved to discover that he treated her very well and was fair and patient. Over the past month, she was learning her craft quickly and Thomas seemed pleased with her progress.

The apartment in which Thomas resided was directly above the clothing shop he owned, and a dark, steep staircase connected the two. Thomas' tenement had only three rooms: a kitchen, main room, and bedroom. Elaisse slept in a tiny single bed in the corner of the main room.

She wondered how Thomas' family had found room in the tiny apartment before his wife died many years ago, and before his son had gone to war in France. She knew it wasn't her place to ask personal questions and he didn't volunteer any information about his family.

Still, she liked Thomas and appreciated his kindness. She got used to his bushy gray eyebrows and his piercing eyes that always gave him a fierce demeanor, because she soon learned that his personality was much nicer than his appearance. He was arthritic, and she felt useful because he quickly became dependent upon her thin, nimble fingers to securely sew the clothing.

Elaisse was beginning to settle into a daily routine of opening the shop for customers and taking measurements of their sizes. She would retreat into the little room behind the main sales shop and choose between hundreds of spools of thread and dozens of rolls of colorful cloth as she would begin to create sturdy garments, stitching with great care.

But then things changed.

She felt that life was beginning to unravel, just as her garments would if they were not sewn properly.

The sickness had arrived in London.

The tell-tale signs began subtly. A few less customers here, a few more rumors there.

Then the pace began to quicken. Elaisse noticed that people began wearing handkerchiefs over their noses and mouths, and they filled their pockets with sweet-smelling herbs. They refused to shake hands, and avoided displays of grief as they mourned lost loved ones, and others retreated into the dark holes of their tenements to grieve alone. Every so often, someone would stand in the streets and read Bible verses to the passers-by, not caring if no one listened.

But the worst was the man with the push-cart that traveled the streets of London once a week.

"Bring out your dead!"

The call would reverberate through the streets, and Elaisse cringed when she heard it. She never looked out the garment shop window to see the man with the push-cart, so her imagination about him ran wild.

In her mind, the man pushing the wagon was an evil monster, drooling over how many dead people he could gather, and clenching his yellowed, sharpened teeth in glee over the lifeless, stiff bodies piled high in his cart.

Whether or not her mental picture of the push-cart man was accurate, Elaisse was determined not to investigate. On the day of the collection, she would hide in terror behind the sales counter until the wagonload of dead bodies passed.

And so the days continued, some good, some not so good.

Her increasing awareness of the pestilence made life very stressful. Every morning when she awoke, she would fearfully inspect her armpits for any signs of the pestilence. She couldn't take a breath until she was positive she was spared the surety of death for one more day.

On this particular morning in early December, her armpits were smooth once again. She felt her knees grow weak with relief and she began to breathe normally as she got out of bed.

She could hear Thomas, who was cooking their breakfast in the small apartment kitchen right next to her bed. Privacy was nonexistent in the tiny tenement, and Elaisse reached for the chamber pot by her bed.

Still wearing her flannel bedclothes, she took the chamber pot to the stairs where she relieved herself in the darkness of the steep stairwell. She replaced the full chamber pot when she was finished, and went back into the stairwell to change her clothes. Then she came back into the apparent, fully dressed for her day.

"Throw it out the window," Thomas told her, nodding at the chamber pot that still contained her urine. Sighing, Elaisse realized that she would never get used to the unsanitary conditions of everyday life in London.

She purposely avoided looking out into the street when she threw the contents of the chamber pot below. She wanted to remain in the world of the apartment, and not witness anything happening outside in the world of the city.

There was that baby crying again. She could hear the baby who lived in the apartment next door. Many of the buildings in the city were built rapidly and with questionable materials, so often the walls were thin. The walls in Thomas' tenement were no exception.

She briefly wondered why the baby's mother didn't see to the infant and stop the crying. Usually, she could hear the mother being attentive to the child. But now the baby sounded decidedly unhappy. Elaisse decided it was not her problem.

She joined Thomas at the table and ate the stone-ground,

rough breakfast bread and the hot gruel that accompanied it. She poured herself a glass of murky water from the pitcher; milk was getting scarce. Because of the rampant sickness, supplies of nearly everything were becoming difficult to locate at any price.

After breakfast, she and Thomas traveled down the dark, narrow stairs and began the routine of opening the garment shop. Thomas raised the curtain at the front window and Elaisse lit the candles on the walls. Dress-making mannequins were positioned to show off the material at the best angles, and the tray holding the coins was placed under the counter.

On that morning, they had a long wait for their first customer. Elaisse was busy in the back room, sewing the seams of a tunic, when she heard a woman enter the shop. Feeling nosy, she peeked into the sales area.

"How are you today?" asked Thomas of his customer.

Elaisse couldn't keep from spying. Hiding behind the back wall, she watched the customer. She was looking for any signs of illness in the woman. But this woman appeared healthy, and therefore harmless. She appeared to be a woman of means, but was in obvious distress.

"I'd like a shroud sewn," the woman told Thomas.

Thomas hesitated. Then he softly said, "We don't sew shrouds here. Perhaps you might visit Mr. Redfield, the nearest undertaker. His office is only five shops down, on this very street."

To Elaisse's dismay and embarrassment, the woman burst into tears.

"No!" the woman cried out. "Don't you know? I've already been there! Mr. Redfield is dead. I have money. I can pay you anything!"

Elaisse gasped, and almost gave herself away. Mr. Redfield dead! The pestilence was getting closer and closer.

"I can't do anything for you," Thomas said, his hands outspread, palms upwards.

The woman seemed to calm herself. "My son is dead," she said, speaking through her grief. "He was barely eleven years old.

It was a horrible and painful death. But he was a good boy so God will take him. I want to send my son to his Maker properly, in a burial shroud."

Thomas was still standing in front of the woman, appearing miserably undecided. Suddenly Elaisse felt duty-bound to speak for him.

She stepped out unhesitatingly into the sales room. "We'll help you," she said, and Thomas swiveled his head to look at her in surprise. "How tall was your son? About four feet, you say? Please come back tomorrow morning. You'll have your shroud."

Elaisse saw the woman off. When the lady had gone, she turned to Thomas.

"We have to help her. Mr. Redfield is dead," she said simply.

Instead of losing his temper, Thomas sighed and said, "You're right. The world is changing, and we must change with it."

Elaisse was noticing that Thomas seemed to be deferring to her decisions as of late. With the tensions of witnessing all of the sickness and death in the city, Thomas was becoming increasingly timid and indecisive. Giving him a smile to silently thank him for helping the woman who had lost her son, she turned to enter the back room.

That was the day that Elaisse learned how to make a burial shroud.

When evening came, and there were no other customers, it was time to call it a day. They trudged up the stairs back to the tiny apartment. When they entered the main room, Elaisse could hear the baby crying again from next door.

"Maybe we should find out what's wrong with that baby," Elaisse said.

"It's none of our business," Thomas said.

"Something is wrong."

"Everything is wrong."

"But it's a baby."

Thomas sighed, deferring to her once again. "All right, I suppose one of us ought to investigate."

"Let's go together," Elaisse said. "We'll have to go through the bake shop next door."

They each took a candle and went back down the dark staircase, the flames creating shadows that moved eerily upon the walls. The steps were steep and the stairwell was very narrow. Elaisse felt afraid, not of the darkness, but of the unknown that was waiting next door.

They went into the street, then walked to the bake shop. The entrance door was locked.

"Break it down," she told him.

He didn't argue. Thomas kicked in the door of the bake shop. It was dark and silent inside, and appeared deserted.

Elaisse wondered, *How could this shop be vacant if there is a baby crying upstairs? The baby's parents have to be here somewhere. Don't they?*

She asked Thomas, "Do you remember the last time this bake shop was open?"

He shrugged. "Maybe two days ago."

They looked at each other, searching each other's faces for answers, then looked back inside the dark bake shop. Finally Elaisse stepped inside and Thomas followed.

They found a stairwell almost identical to the one in their own shop. They began to climb the stairs, taking one step at a time, quietly dreading having to face whatever waited for them at the top of the narrow staircase.

When they reached the top, Elaisse pushed the apartment door and was surprised at how easily it opened. The apartment was completely dark, and she lifted the candle so she could view her surroundings.

Thomas entered the room right behind her, and his candle was also lifted. The flickering candles gave off barely enough light for them to see details of the room in which they were standing. Moving shadows were everywhere, seeming to have a life of their own.

Suddenly Elaisse realized that it wasn't just the candlelight shadows that moved along the walls. Something was truly moving inside the apartment.

And at that moment, she recognized the source of the motion.

Rats!

The rats were startled by the presence of two humans holding brightly lit candles, and they rushed to find dark places to hide. Elaisse could see their fat, stubby bodies covered with dark, mottled fur and the long tails that trailed behind them like whipcords. She could hear the scraping of their little claws on the wooden floor as the rodents scurried, climbing over each other in their hurry to find concealment.

Her heart leaped into her mouth, and she almost dropped her candleholder. "Oh!" she cried in disgust.

At the sound of her voice, the baby began crying again from the other room. Thomas stood uncertainly. But Elaisse went into action, and rushed to the bedroom door. Her hands reached the knob, turned it and then flung the door wide open.

She stood in the doorway of the bedroom, sickened by the terrible smell, her candle held high. She called to Thomas, "Bring your candle! I need to see more clearly."

He appeared at her side, and together they held up their candles.

Elaisse saw the bed where two people lay prone, very close to each other. She thought it was a man and a woman, but she couldn't be sure because both of their faces seemed unnaturally dark. The eye sockets appeared to be black and empty because the eyes were sunken into the skulls.

But what horrified Elaisse the most was what little remained of the noses of the two people on the bed.

She turned away. Gulping air, fighting to keep her stomach from coming up through her throat in a fit of intense nausea, she held her position until her sickness passed.

Finally sure she was not going to vomit, she turned back and looked at Thomas, who was still staring at the dead couple with morbid fascination.

The noses of the dead people had been gnawed away by rats. The ears were also gone. Only the heads of the victims were visible. Their bodies were under blankets, mercifully covering any other damage the rats might have done.

Elaisse's gaze left the two dead victims and traveled over the rest of the room. There was a crib next to the bed. She walked over and looked inside, not knowing if she was prepared for whatever condition she might find the infant.

But it was alive, and when the baby saw her, it started to wail once again. It seemed that the rats had only decimated the two people on the bed who were already dead, because the child appeared to be untouched. But how much longer would the rats have gone before they decided to advance upon this poor child?

How long would it have taken the rats before they would have crawled over the infant with their clawed feet as their naked, scaly tails trailed behind? How long would the rats have waited to begin to feed upon this tiny baby who would have been unable to defend itself against the long, sharp teeth?

And then another, worse question arose in Elaisse's thoughts. Was this child sick with the pestilence? Would touching the infant bring the illness upon both herself and Thomas?

Nonsense, she scolded herself. *The pestilence is brought on by an act of God to punish the people. Besides, everyone knows the pestilence is spread by invisible devils in bad air. You can't catch it from other people.*

Still, she hesitated, wondering if you could indeed get it from other people, but the baby continued to cry. Then Elaisse decided that if the child could cry, it must not be sick.

She reached into the crib and picked up the infant. She brought it to her chest and covered it with the blanket she took from the crib. "Let's go back now," she told Thomas.

Once in Thomas' apartment, Elaisse placed the baby on her bed, and gently unwrapped the blanket so she could examine the infant. It was a boy of about three months of age; he seemed all right except for a little dehydration and a lot of hunger. Elaisse frowned at the boy's little ribs because they were visible in his chest. *How long has it been since this child had any nourishment?* she silently wondered. *How long has he been in a room with two dead people?*

She said to Thomas, "I have to go back next door to retrieve a nursing bottle. We need to give this baby some water right away, and then find some cow's milk."

"No, don't go next door again," Thomas told her. "I'll go. Then I'll be the one to go find some milk. It'll be difficult to find, but I won't give up until I do."

Elaisse was surprised but grateful for Thomas' sudden assertiveness. She hadn't seen him take charge in weeks.

She felt hope that somehow things would turn out all right and this nightmare would end; after all, she was holding a new life in her arms that had somehow survived the most abhorrent conditions. She took it as a sign. If the baby could come out of this horrible pestilence almost unscathed, then perhaps she and Thomas could as well.

All through the night, Elaisse cared for the infant. When the baby was finally sated with milk and ready to sleep, she put the little boy in her own bed and sat in a chair beside it. She softly hummed as she sewed the burial shroud for the customer who had lost her son.

Elaisse fell asleep in the chair, the completed burial shroud limp in her lap. Then the sun cast its first rays upon the clearing sky, and the window allowed some light to penetrate the apartment. The baby began to stir and she attended to the little boy. She fed the infant and wrapped him warmly in his little blanket.

Thomas came out of the bedroom and began the day's routine. When breakfast was finished, he and Elaisse traveled back down the stairwell so they could open the garment shop. The only difference this day was from any other was that now Elaisse carried a baby in her arms.

When Thomas went to the front of the shop to open the curtain, Elaisse saw the woman who needed the shroud waiting outside. Thomas opened the door and let her in. The woman appeared wan and shaken.

The woman began talking to Thomas, then her conversation

drifted off when she saw that Elaisse had a baby. "Please, can I hold him for a minute?" the woman asked through fresh tears. "It would be a great comfort to me."

"Of course," Elaisse said, coming over to the woman. She gently placed the baby into the woman's arms.

And then it all fell into place. Elaisse suddenly understood that these two needed each other. "His parents are dead, so I don't know his name. I suppose you can name him."

"What?" The woman looked at Elaisse incredulously.

"I work in this shop with Thomas," Elaisse explained. "I never leave here. I don't think this would be a very good life for a baby, because I couldn't give him very much attention. Another thing—there are rats in this building. I'd be afraid the rats would come after this little boy some time when I couldn't watch out for him. This poor baby has been through enough already. I think he'd have a better home with you than with anything I could give him. Don't you agree? Would you like to have him, and to be his mother?"

The woman appeared speechless for a moment, then exclaimed, "May the Lord God bless you! I'll take good care of this little one. I'll get him out of London. I'll be moving him to Yorkshire today, where I am to meet my husband."

And so the woman took both the shroud and the baby, and left the shop.

Thomas looked at Elaisse. "Do you always make such bold decisions?"

She smiled. "I guess I do. I am learning to think for myself, as Roger told me I should."

"You mean that unhinged young man who escorted you?"

This time she laughed out loud. "Yes, that's the one."

Chapter Six

The bishop felt remorse for his actions, but did them anyway.

He knew that to leave his flock in this time of dire need was cowardice. He packed a small traveling bag, ashamed of his deficiencies yet feeling powerless to change. He couldn't bear to look into one more desperately ill face, to read the Catholic rites over one more diseased body, or to mouth the religious words in which he no longer believed.

As bishop of Saint Paul's Cathedral, he resided over the largest church in London. One by one, he had watched his priests sicken and die terrible deaths. He had searched inwardly for reasons why all of this tragedy was taking place, but he only found his faith waning and his soul wanting.

Sadly he continued to pack, even though he knew there were people waiting in the church who were hoping to receive his prayers. He ignored them; he couldn't bear to face them.

Times of trouble tended to bring out the real person that was within everyone. In himself, the real person was self-centered and cowardly. He intended to sneak out the back door of the church and to flee London.

As he began to button up his satchel, a piece of parchment paper fell out and fluttered to the floor. The bishop ignored it, and walked away, leaving the paper on the floor of the rectory.

The paper contained a message that was delivered just that very morning. It was from the church leaders, and it said:

Because the pestilence is so wide-spread, many people are left without priests to give God's comfort to the living and to issue the Holy Sacraments to the

73

dying. Therefore, we decree that if men are near death without the presence of a priest, they now have the permission of the church to make confessions to each other. If fate deems it that no men are present, then the dying may make confessions to a woman, or even to children who are beyond the age of twelve. We are, in these desperate times, giving the layperson the ability and the permission to acquire the ears of God, which would normally be sanctified only from ordained priests.

The bishop had obviously agreed with the letter, because now he was gone. The people waiting patiently in the church for his prayers waited in vain.

January 1349

Elaisse witnessed the world falling apart before her eyes. God appeared to be unleashing a terrible vengeance upon all people. Was this the end of mankind that Revelations had so chillingly foretold?

And now, in the January of a new year, in the home of Thomas Taylor, Elaisse sat in a bedside chair watching her mentor die.

She knew there was nothing she could do for him except to keep him company and to try to soothe his fears. She also knew that her apprenticeship contract in no way obligated her to see her teacher through to his death, but morally she felt she should. And besides, she had nowhere else to go.

As Elaisse sat by Thomas' bedside hour after hour, she did a lot of contemplating. She thought of her parents and her friends, left behind in the country. Had they survived the pestilence? Her parents were wealthy, but money didn't buy health.

Dawn lightened the room, and she wiped Thomas' forehead with a damp cloth. He burned with heat, and moaned for water. When Elaisse tried to help him drink from a glass, Thomas couldn't seem to make his swollen tongue function, and the water dribbled uselessly down his chin. Dark blotches were beginning to form on his cheeks, and periodically his body jerked in spasms as his nervous system went awry. He sighed and lay back against his pillow, and she resumed wiping his brow with the cloth.

She had sought a doctor, but none were to be found. Previously she had ridiculed the bird-like beaks of their masks, but now she wished she had their expertise. Priests were equally absent.

She was on her own to nurse Thomas.

She sat back on her chair and continued to meditate. How trivial life's everyday problems appeared now, compared to all of this. She wished she had had more perspective earlier, but it was better now than never.

She remembered the joy she had experienced in her life. She wished she had foreseen how fleeting joy could be. If she had known what was to come, she certainly would have made the most of it while any joy was happening. Oh, how she had taken her life for granted! She regretted her restraint. How unnecessarily she had followed the rules that society dictated so closely, rarely questioning their purpose.

And those rules—most of the old rules in life seemed to be meaningless now, including the distinction between the social classes. It had been so important to her father that servants be kept in their place. Her father had always told her that she was superior to peasants due to her upper-class lineage. Now she only had to glance around the city to be aware that the pestilence was not particular as to social status. In the Great Dying, everyone was considered an equal opportunity for which death could stake its claim.

She realized that she had not thought of her father in a very long time.

So many thoughts ran through her mind as the sun continued to fill the room with light. How odd it was that the sun would continue to shine daily, but all things made of flesh might cease.

And if all the people in the world were to die, the sun would rise and set upon an empty landscape. Houses would fall and fields would be reclaimed by wilderness. Would anything be of any consequence if the only life forms that could comprehend the meaning of life were no longer around to contemplate it? Or was that an arrogant position, to take the stance that nothing was important in the world if humans were not part of it?

Elaisse thought of her own mortality. She had recently turned seventeen; her birthday passing without celebration. Would she not see eighteen? Were her days numbered? Was she ready to face death, to discover what, if anything, lay beyond?

She realized that once she was faced with the possibility of no choice, she seemed resigned to fate. A week ago, she would have been terrified to think that death could be stalking her. But now, it was strange to discover that she was actually getting used to the idea that she could die at any time. How much more could the mind get used to when exposed to such abhorrent circumstances?

Suddenly she heard a commotion coming from the street below. Another group of flagellants was approaching. Elaisse went to the second-story window in the room and peered to the street below. She could see the band of about fifty people coming in an odd procession from around the corner.

Elaisse knew that flagellants were penitents. They were fanatics who took it upon themselves to give penance for the sins of the rest of the world. They had the hopes that by doing this, God would provide forgiveness and spare His children from the Great Dying.

Their actions were abhorrent to watch; yet Elaisse could not seem to pull herself away from the window. The penitents repeatedly thrashed and flogged themselves or others within their group, all the time singing mournful religious songs. Women ran beside the men and caught any spilled blood in their hands, then rubbed the blood over their faces. Some of the flagellants would strip to the waist in order for the beatings to strike naked flesh. They seemed unmindful of the severe chill of winter, and only replaced their coats during breaks in the floggings.

This group of flagellants had cat-o-nine-tails knotted with

nails on the end. Their blood flowed freely. They beat themselves and exposed their flesh to the elements in extreme demonstrations of martyrdom. They beseeched bystanders to join them, telling London's citizens that giving penance was mankind's only hope of salvation.

Elaisse could not stop herself from staring. She was mesmerized by the hysteria happening below. Each flagellant appeared to be trying to outdo the others in his or her degree of suffering.

Elaisse wondered, *Why would perfectly healthy people choose to make themselves sick, when there were so many who had no choice but to be sick and wished to be well?*

Had everyone in the world lost his or her senses and gone mad?

She was glad when the flagellants rounded the corner and disappeared from her view. Soon their penitent noise was gone as well. Sighing, Elaisse went back to her deathwatch of Thomas Taylor.

He was beginning to smell very bad. All of the toxins from deep within his body seemed to be rising to the surface. Boils and pustules oozed foulness and his high temperature was a catalyst to project the smells into the room. She couldn't stand the stench any longer; she went back to the window and opened it to let the outside air enter the room.

Thoughts raced through her brain unchecked and unwanted. All her life she had been told that during times of sickness, windows should be locked tightly. The reasoning behind this was that sick people were more susceptible to bad air, and besides, everyone knew that invisible evil devils traveled unnoticed through the air.

But now when she took deep breaths of the outside air, it seemed to make her feel better, not worse. Certainly the outside air seemed to ease the nausea she felt when she breathed Thomas' foul stench. Should everything she had been told about open windows be discarded? What was fact and what was fiction?

She decided that if she ever survived the Great Dying, she would change the way she lived her life. She evaluated the superstitions of her old life with the things she had been learning from her new one. She decided that she would dismiss everything she had been told and start over. What was it that Roger told her? That she needed to think for herself.

Elaisse looked at Thomas. She felt her heart freeze in her chest at what she saw.

He was sitting up, his mouth gaping, the skin melting off the bones of his face before her very eyes. He threw back the covers, revealing bedclothes that were stuck to his skin from the oozing, open sores and from the rancid sweat of his body.

A bony arm covered in boils and black blotches stretched out as he pointed directly at her. "You're next," he croaked, "you're next!"

Thomas dragged himself out of the bed, and stood on unsteady bare feet. Still pointing his finger, he lurched toward her.

"You will be just like me!" he cried as he reached her. Elaisse tried to get up from her chair, but Thomas grabbed her shoulders with his bony, diseased fingers and then with stinking, rotted breath, he said, "You already are like me!"

Elaisse woke with a start.

Her heart raced in her chest; pounded against her ribs. It was only a dream, and yet she had to use all her will to force herself to look at the bedridden man across the room.

Thomas was not getting out of bed and coming for her.

Thomas was dead, lying still and silent under the covers. The large, dark buboes that had strained the skin underneath his armpits had burst, darkening the blanket with blood.

"Oh!" Elaisse cried and ran from Thomas' room. She lay upon her own small bed in a corner of the main room and sobbed. She was exhausted and depressed. She needed to purge the sorrow from her system so that she could think about what she should do next.

Her body demanded rest, and she gave in. Dreams of her

home in the country were so vivid that she felt she could smell the green meadows and hear the birds sing. When she awoke, she thought, *Why did I leave?*

And then she realized, *It's because I didn't know any better. And I had no idea the great turns fate could take. If I survive the Great Dying, I will make sure some good comes out if this. And when I can travel, I'm going home.*

From the angle of the sun, she estimated she had been sleeping for about two hours. She figured it was around noon.

And then she realized something. Had she missed the man with the death wagon? When was the last time she had heard the gruesome call of the man who removed the dead bodies from the streets of London? *Bring out your dead!*

She couldn't leave London until Thomas Taylor was buried. She knew she couldn't simply leave him lying in his bed to rot. Even though she no longer believed that God caused the pestilence, she still believed in God. Therefore, she needed to find a priest to bless Thomas and to ensure that he held passage into Heaven.

That meant, if the man with the push-cart was not going to come to her, she must venture out into the streets and go to him. She would find him and summon him back to this house. Otherwise...well, she wouldn't think like that.

She grabbed a woolen cloak and went outside. The streets were dirtier than ever. The men who were paid by the city to rake up the muck had obviously been absent for a long while. Chickens roamed freely and here and there, a few children wandered. But other than those few children, the street was strangely deserted of people.

Which way to go? Elaisse went north, choosing the direction at random. She walked a few steps when out of a dark doorstep, a bedraggled boy of about ten or eleven years old came forth.

"Would you have a sixpence?" the child asked.

Elaisse dug in her satchel for a coin. "Where're your parents?"

"Dead," the child said. "All of my family are dead. It's the

Jews, you know."

She was startled. She didn't think she had heard him correctly.

"The Jews!" the boy continued. "The Jews poisoned the wells! That's why everyone is dying!"

Elaisse was baffled. Was everyone losing their mind? She understood how impotent people must feel, and perhaps that could make them place blame upon something tangible. She knew from stories that historically, people of the Jewish faith had been the scapegoats of many natural disasters. But how often had the Jews really been responsible for the tragedies of the world? Once, twice, never? Elaisse shook her head. Rubbish. It was all rubbish.

She felt a need to set this child straight. "Listen," she said, "people are dying everywhere, not just in London. How could it be possible for the Jews to poison every well at every place in England? Think about it! It is *not* possible."

"No! No!" the boy protested loudly. "It is because of the Jews for sure! They murdered Christ. And now they are murdering everyone who obeys Christ."

Disgusted, Elaisse threw a coin into the muck, then went on her way. Out of the corner of her eye, she saw the boy scrabbling upon the ground to retrieve the fallen money.

Continuing her walk down the street, she came across an elderly woman, all draped in shawls. The woman was making her way slowly, hunched and shuffling.

"Have you seen the wagon that carries off the dead?" Elaisse asked her.

"Gone. There are no more carts to carry off the dead," the woman said. "Probably the one who pushed the cart is dead himself."

"But there is a dead man in the house where I'm staying," Elaisse said, "and he needs to be taken care of."

"Even if the cart-pusher were still taking corpses, where would your dead man be buried? There are no graveyards left that are not already overflowing with bodies. I hear the dead are even being thrown into the Thames. And priests! Well, I haven't seen one in weeks. The churches are empty, save for the sick who are praying for their own salvation, because there are no priests to do it for them," the woman said as she shook her head sadly. "Go home. You cannot find help for your dead man. Go home and worry about yourself."

Elaisse was stunned. She tended to believe this old woman. It felt like the truth. There would be no one to help her.

And so Elaisse went back to the house of her dead teacher. She climbed the stairs over the garment shop and went into the main room. She sat on her little bed in the corner and did some more thinking.

Who would bury Thomas Taylor?

The answer was obvious.

She would.

Now would be the time to utilize the sewing skills she had learned. She went to a cabinet and retrieved a fresh sheet and sewed it into a shroud. She took a wash basin and filled it with water. She mustered up her courage and entered Thomas's bedroom. Gently she washed him with a sponge. His eyes were half closed, and the irises seemed to peek out from beneath the lids. It was as though he was watching her efforts, as if he was thinking, *Be kind to me.*

While she sponged the blood and pus off of his face and neck, she didn't cry. She felt empty of tears. She cleaned him off the best she could, then covered him with her makeshift shroud.

When she was done, the sun was setting. She went back to her bed and fell into an exhausted sleep, and did not dream.

The next morning, the sky was overcast, dark and foreboding. How appropriate that the weather would reflect the mood of the city. Elaisse went back into the street.

She wandered for awhile, searching for an abandoned cart. Finding one, she pushed it back to Thomas' house and left it at the doorstep of the garment store on the first floor. Going back up the stairs, Elaisse realized that it would be difficult to maneuver his body down the stairs. Perhaps she could drag him with the help of gravity.

Grunting and straining with her efforts, Elaisse dragged Thomas down the stairs. At the bottom, she rested for a minute. Sweat streamed down her temples and stung her eyes. But then she took a deep breath and continued to drag poor Thomas across the garment shop and to the door.

Once at the doorstep, she realized how enormous a task it would be to lift Thomas into the cart. After a few tries, she decided that she just couldn't do it alone.

She began walking back down the street, searching for someone to help. Out of the corner of her eye she saw a movement, and turned around to face the same ten-year-old bedraggled boy that she had chanced upon the day before.

"Would you have another sixpence?" the child asked again, recognizing her.

"I'll give you a whole shilling if you'll help me," Elaisse tempted him.

His eyes widened. Then he became suspicious. "What would I have to do?"

"I need to lift a dead man into a cart," Elaisse said. "You can have a whole shilling for only a minute's work if you'll help me."

"It's the Jews, you know," the boy said.

"Listen, you." Elaisse strained to hold her temper in check. "I don't want to hear about any Jews poisoning any wells. I just want my teacher lifted into a cart. Do you want the shilling or not?"

"Sure, I'll lift your dead man," the boy said, "but let me see the shilling first."

She showed it to him, and he followed her to where poor Thomas waited in his makeshift shroud. Together they pushed and pulled, and got the body on board the cart.

"Thank you," Elaisse told the boy.

"I do what I have to do to survive," the boy said, "so I don't wind up like your dead man. I can do anything you need for a sixpence."

Elaisse gave the boy the coin and he ran off.

She pushed the cart towards the nearest church. In the church courtyard, she saw it was just as the old woman had told her, that the graveyard was full. She saw mass graves that still had not been covered with earth, and which laid open to reveal multitudes of bodies inside, piled all the way to the top of the holes.

Pulling Thomas off the cart, she dragged him to an open grave. She pushed him into the hole, and his body fell stiffly on top of countless other victims. Mournfully she said a prayer, not knowing if God could hear her.

"I'm sorry it has to end like this, Thomas," she told him. "This is the best I can do for you. I'm so very, very sorry. I hope you find peace."

Chapter Seven

The bacterium *Yersinia pestis* found perfect conditions for its spread throughout London.

Rats roamed the streets freely, taking their infected fleas from dwelling to dwelling. All over in the crowded and stinking tenements, people would go to sleep at night appearing healthy, only to awaken the next morning bearing the telltale buboes.

Fear was the predominant emotion; for although medieval Londoners were well acquainted with mysterious diseases caused by their living conditions, never had death been so unrestrained in its rampage. Death became an obsession of the people, and the ones that didn't flee the city were reduced to cowering in fright.

The graveyards in the church courtyards quickly filled, and the few bishops and priests that remained in London raced against time to consecrate more ground for new places to bury the dead. Services were held for multiple deceased, and funerals were held back to back to accommodate the ever-increasing numbers of the dead.

London became a city of horrors.

Animals that were not yet sick had no one to feed them, so some fed upon their dead masters. Healthy babies, with no one to look after them, starved in their cribs. Many people who weren't sick ran away. Husbands left wives, and mothers left children.

Of the healthy people that remained, some paid penance by living frugally, while others partied freely, drinking and dancing. Social structures fell apart and eventually law enforcement became non-existent.

Then the rains came.

The seemingly unending downpours washed some streets clean, but pooled in others, creating cesspools of filth and breeding bacteria. Orphaned children still roamed the streets, and too often the ones that were spared from the pestilence died anyway of dysentery or cholera from the dirty rainwater.

All the while, the rats traveled from dwelling to dwelling.

Early February 1349

It rained for days.

Elaisse found herself spending the days in her bed, sleeping too much in her attempts to block out the daily tragedies that went on right outside her window. When she wasn't sleeping, she roamed the apartment; traveling in tight circles as she wandered throughout the tiny tenement. Eventually she ran out of food, and she knew she'd have to venture back out into the street to search for more.

The next day the rain stopped. Hungry, Elaisse decided that now would be the time to go back out to the street.

Were there any shops open? She doubted it. She didn't know where she could locate more food, but all that mattered was that she did.

She took a deep breath as she once again grabbed her woolen cloak, and thought to herself, *I'm taking this one step at a time. This is my new life, and although I may not be able to change what happens in the future, perhaps I can do something about today.*

She went out the door of the garment shop. Had it really only been three days since she had taken Thomas for his last journey through this doorway? It seemed like a lifetime ago.

She realized that it was already February. Perhaps the new month would prove to be more benevolent than the last. In any case, Elaisse knew that her task on this first day of February would be to locate a food source.

She walked down the street, hoping she would not run into

the young, bedraggled boy that had held such malevolence against the Jews. She peered into the windows of the shops as she walked. Some were boarded up, but others were simply empty and abandoned. Where was everybody? Surely not everyone had died or left London—had they?

But it seemed as though nearly all had. The only people she saw were mostly the very young and the very old. She came across an elderly man who sat in the open doorway of a fish store. He was pale and gaunt, with a large nose and very crooked teeth.

"May I buy some fish?" Elaisse asked him.

"None fresh," the man said.

"How about salted?" Her stomach growled. "Or dried?"

The old man scrutinized her, then smiled, revealing his awful teeth. "It'll be expensive."

Elaisse thanked God that she still had money left. "I have enough."

"Come in then," the old man said. "My name is Edmund, and I'm the fishmonger on this block. At least I used to be, when there were people around to buy my fish. So who might you be?"

She told him her real name, figuring there was no longer any reason to hide, and he said, "All right, Elaisse. You can have three fish for a pound."

"A pound!" Elaisse exclaimed. "That's a terrible price!"

"Take it or leave it. And if you take it, don't ask for more. I can't sell you any more than three fish or else I'll starve myself." The man went to his counter and retrieved three small and shriveled dried fish.

She was too hungry to argue, and the man knew it. "I'll take it," she told him.

She took the fish that he wrapped in paper. She left his store, but went only another block before hunger overcame her. She ducked into a dark and deserted doorway and opened the paper wrapping. The fish were hard and chewy, but Elaisse wolfed all three of them down, one right after the other.

It was cold, so very cold. Elaisse could see her own breath.

She pulled her woolen cloak tighter around herself, and was thankful that her shoes had very thick soles. She tried to walk near the buildings, because the centers of the streets were thick with mud.

She approached another shop that had an open door. The lighting inside was very dim, but the store didn't appear deserted, as did most others. She poked her head inside the doorway, and cried, "Hello? Is anybody here?"

There was no answer. She tentatively stepped inside, looking around. Food! Here was food. It was a butcher shop. She could tell because a lamb was tied in the corner and chickens roamed freely throughout the store.

"Hello?" she called again.

Elaisse stepped over to the counter, then gasped. On the floor behind the counter was a man lying in a pool of blood. Only this man had not died of the pestilence. This man had a large knife protruding from his chest.

"Oh!" Elaisse cried, and fled back out into the street. Once there, she gulped great breaths of air, trying to calm her stomach, which threatened to give up the three fish inside. Then she composed herself. After all, why should observing death by murder be any more frightening than witnessing death by disease?

So she went back into the butcher shop, taking great care not to look at the dead proprietor sprawled on the floor behind the counter. She rummaged around, in search of prepared meat. There was none to be found. Obviously the person who had murdered the man behind the counter had the same idea about finding meat.

But then she pulled out a drawer and was rewarded for her diligence by finding strips of mutton jerky inside. Elaisse sighed in relief. There were enough of the hard, dried meat strips to last for a few days if she were careful. She began stuffing her pockets with the jerky.

The bleating of the lamb caught her attention. Tied to the wall, she knew it would surely starve.

So then … could she butcher the lamb? Would it eventually come to that?

Sighing, she untied the lamb and set it loose. It ran out of the door and off into the street. She couldn't bring herself to kill the lamb. But chickens—maybe she could butcher a chicken. She didn't know why she felt able to kill one type of animal and not another. Maybe it was because chickens didn't possess the large, mournful eyes as did the lamb. Poor chickens. It was not their fault that they weren't born cute.

She grabbed one of the hens that scavenged among the floorboards of the store. Before she could give herself time to think about what she was doing, Elaisse took it into the back room of the store where the butchering equipment was located. Quickly she chopped off its head, then proceeded to strip it of feathers. She took the chicken back to Thomas' house and boiled it for soup.

All in all, it had been a successful day, because she had accomplished what she set out to do. She thanked God that she had survived another day. But now it was time to make plans to leave London.

She was quite certain that she wouldn't be able to find an escort to help her travel home, even though conventional appropriateness dictated that no woman should travel without one. But nothing was conventional in these times, appropriate or not.

At least she figured she still had her horse. In fact, horses seemed to be almost immune from the pestilence, whereas other animals such as pigs were not. Elaisse had no way of knowing that it was because fleas were repelled by horses' scents. Her horse was housed in the common stable on the street corner.

She decided she would attempt to travel back to where she came from—Wynham Castle—on her own. She felt that if she didn't try to travel, she could either starve or wind up murdered like the butcher shop proprietor. She had heard vague stories that other things could happen to women.

All of those things were supposing she avoided the sickness, which was certainly no guarantee, either. So—what would she have to lose by trying to make her way back to Wynham alone? She could die on the road traveling, but she could die as well if she stayed in Thomas' tenement apartment.

She went back to her little bed and drifted off to sleep in the corner of the main room. Suddenly she was awakened by a *crash!*

It seemed to have come from the garment shop on the floor below. Elaisse sat up, frozen in fright. The noise sounded as though something had been knocked over onto the floor.

There was someone in the garment shop!

She realized that it must be very late, because the room was enveloped in darkness. She cursed the fact that she had not lit a candle before she went to bed. Straining to listen for any sound, Elaisse held her breath as she sat on her bed.

More sounds were not long in coming. She could hear somebody rummaging through the store below. Objects were flung on the floor and against the walls. Whoever was raiding the store did not seem to care if he or she was to be discovered in the act. But why should the person care? Law enforcement would not come to the rescue.

And then she wondered, *Will the intruder be satisfied with the store, or will he or she come upstairs?* Elaisse didn't know, and couldn't take the chance that the intruder would simply go away. It was flight or fight, and since she couldn't jump out the second story window, her only option was to fight.

She threw the covers off and jumped out of bed. She ran to the kitchen and grabbed the biggest knife she could find. Unmindful of the fact that she was shaking, Elaisse stood perched just inside the doorway, which led into the main room from the stairs. She listened and waited.

There! Another sound, closer now. As she had feared, the intruder was coming up the stairs, slowly and meticulously.

Elaisse raised the knife to head-level, aiming it, and holding it with both hands. She wanted to make her first thrust a good one. She did not want to learn the intruder's identity beforehand. She would kill first, then discover who it was later.

Certainly whoever was approaching up the stairs was up to no good. For weeks, she had struggled to survive. She sometimes acted on instinct instead of with thought. Her instinct was telling her now that whoever this intruder was, he or she was dangerous, and Elaisse had to either kill or be killed.

The intruder was close. The door creaked open.

Now! Elaisse shoved the knife downwards, catching the intruder just as he put his head through the doorway. The knife went into the man's upper chest, and Elaisse kept pushing with all her strength, until the knife was imbedded all the way up to its handle. He screamed in surprise, then made a gurgling sound, then dropped straight down into a heap on the floor.

Elaisse watched and waited for a while until she was convinced that the intruder must be dead. She stood over him, panting from her exertion.

Then she went to retrieve a candle and held it up to the man so she could see him. He was a man of medium height. He was scruffy, with uncombed black hair. He was dressed in mismatched clothing. She touched him with her toe to turn his face so that she could look at him.

His face was covered with dark blotches. He had the sickness.

She turned away in horror. She knew the disease was still rampant in the city. Here was more proof that it was time to leave London. Elaisse decided then and there that she would leave for Wynham Castle the first thing in the morning.

She kicked the man as hard as she could. His body fell back down the stairs, loudly tumbling until it reached the bottom of the stairwell.

Elaisse shut the door and stood still for a moment, wondering what to do. She calmed herself, and her shaking ceased. It was just another event in an unpredictable world; a world gone awry.

So she became matter-of-fact, deciding that the excitement was over for now, and simply went back to bed. She lay there, but sleep was long in coming.

She thought back to when she was trying to get to London, and Roger had killed a man in her defense. At the time, she hadn't understood. She thought Roger had performed a criminal act that was sure to summon God's wrath.

But now she was living at the basic level of human existence; on the rudimentary edge of primal impulses. Her desire to survive was surprisingly great. Elaisse had not known before that her will to live could possibly be this strong. She was surprised to find out that she still wanted to live very much indeed.

Just weeks earlier, Elaisse had thought that she was resigned to whatever fate had in store for her, even if it meant death. But today she learned that as long as she still had a choice, she would always choose to live.

She had not gone hunting for a person to kill. The person had come hunting for her. Roger had been right. Here was another area where the old rules didn't apply: it was no sin to kill in self-defense.

Finally she drifted off to sleep, even though she had been sure she wouldn't. Morning came quickly, and her resolve to leave on this very day was even stronger in the sunlight.

She gathered her things, which were just as few as when she had arrived. She used the same satchel as before. It only contained three things that were different from her first trip—less money, strips of mutton jerky, and a large, sharp knife.

Elaisse changed into the cleanest, warmest clothes she had, and braided her hair. She wore a warm hat as protection against the elements. She took her woolen cloak; it would do double duty as a blanket.

She opened the door to the stairwell. Reluctantly she made her way down the steps. The intruder was still at the bottom of the stairs, lying there with his head at an unnatural angle.

She took a deep breath, and then simply stepped over him.

As she passed through the garment store, she saw it was a mess. Clothes and sewing items were strewn every which way. No matter; no one would complain about the lack of order.

She went out the door and into the street for the final time. Elaisse was going back to the country, hoping that the pestilence would be less rampant there. She thought she was going home.

But when she reached the community stable, it seemed too quiet. She entered into the gloom of the large barn-like structure, and her eyes adjusted to the dim light inside.

Where were the horses?

Panicked, Elaisse ran to the stall that should have contained her horse. It was empty.

Slowly, Elaisse sank to her knees in the old, dirty straw that hadn't been mucked in weeks. She put her head in her hands and cried; a keening, wailing sound of defeat. After all she had gone through; here she had thought it was finally over. She had told herself before she had entered the community stable that the worst was behind her, and now she was finding out it wasn't over at all.

The worst was still happening. She had no way to get home.

How much could a single person endure?

No! she thought. *I've come this far. Somehow I will find a way home. I have to collect myself and think.*

She knew she shouldn't waste time or energy wondering what had become of her horse, or of any other horse that was missing from the community stable. Probably they had been stolen by Londoners fleeing the pestilence, or maybe even eaten to ward off starvation. It didn't matter at this point why they were gone; it only mattered that the horses *were* gone.

So Elaisse stopped crying, and stood upright once again. She had come this far, she was still alive, and she couldn't give up. She had to form a plan.

She needed to talk to someone who knew the city from the ground up. She needed to talk to someone who lurked in corners and overheard conversations. She needed to talk to someone who was just as determined to survive as she was; someone who was scrappy and cunning.

She needed to find the beggar child who held such prejudice against the Jews.

Elaisse exited the stable, and blinked in the sunlight. She began walking down the dirty street, peering into empty doorways, and stepping over piles of refuse and filth. There was a foul and sour smell emanating from the garbage strewn over the street, a scent of decay and rot.

But what was even stranger was that the streets seemed completely deserted. Not even chickens roamed amongst the garbage any more, and the usual scavengers such as rats and other vermin were also absent.

Had the entire world died?

Elaisse made her way back to the fishmonger's stall. She wanted to speak to Edmund, to see if he could be of any help. But when she found the tiny shop, Edmund was nowhere around it. Had he stepped out for a moment, or was he gone for good too?

And then she heard a blessed sound from behind. "Could you spare a sixpence?"

Elaisse whirled around, relief flooding through her body. But then she stopped short. It wasn't the beggar boy. Instead, it was an older lad.

"I'll give you a sixpence if you help me find someone," she told the teenager.

"Well, that should be easy, because there aren't a lot of people to choose from," he said.

"Have you seen a ten-year-old boy who tells people that the Jews have poisoned all the wells?"

"Oh, you mean Jonathan. He's eleven, and he does talk about Jews a lot, it seems. Yes, he's over yonder."

"Where is yonder?" Elaisse asked.

"Next street, over there." He pointed. "Now, give me a sixpence, lady."

"Well, you're a cheeky lad, aren't you?" Elaisse dug in her satchel and gave him a sixpence.

"Listen Miss," the teenager said, "times have changed. Or haven't you noticed? You're lucky I'm just a beggar and not a robber."

"I'll keep that in mind," Elaisse told him as she walked away.

She turned the corner and saw a small shadow hiding in a doorway of a deserted Inn. As she approached the Inn, the bedraggled boy of eleven stepped out into the sunlight.

"Well hello, Jonathan," Elaisse greeted him.

"It's the lady who had the dead man," he said in recognition.

"Well, having a dead man only makes me one of many these days, doesn't it?" she said. "I am surprised you haven't asked me for a sixpence. It would be the first time you didn't."

Jonathan grinned and said, "Since you know my name now, I figured you are looking for me, which means you want something. Which also means I will probably get more than a sixpence out of you."

"Can you find a horse for me?"

Jonathan peered intently at her, as though deciding, then said, "I can, but it will cost you two pounds. One for the horse, and one for me."

"What!" Elaisse cried. "No. Two shillings. One for the horse, and one for you."

"No bargaining. Two pounds or no horse. Your choice."

"But two pounds are all I have left," Elaisse wailed, not knowing if revealing that information tipped her bargaining hand or not, and no longer caring. She just felt so desperate, so tired, and so depressed. But she didn't feel defeated. She would never allow herself to feel defeated ever again.

"If you have two pounds left, then you have two pounds to give to me," Jonathan told her. "And you have to pay in advance."

Resigned, she agreed to the boy's terms, outrageous though they were.

"I remember the sewing shop where you and your dead man lived," Jonathan said. "I will meet you there in one hour."

"How do I know you won't take my money and run off with it?" she asked.

"You don't. But do you have a different plan?"

"You're saying I don't have a choice."

"That's right, you don't."

She sighed. "I am asking you, will you please come back, and bring a horse too?"

Jonathan grinned. "Sure I will. If I don't, London is so

deserted that it would be too easy for you to find me again. I'd rather you leave."

She paid him and he turned away, and Elaisse did the same. She went back to Thomas Taylor's store, but she waited at the doorway outside. She wouldn't go into the store, because she knew there was yet another dead man lying inside, at the bottom of the stairs, who had been stabbed by her very own knife.

An hour later, just as promised, Jonathan returned, riding a horse.

Elaisse didn't ask questions, and Jonathan didn't volunteer any information. He dismounted and handed her the reins.

"It's a nag but it will have to do," Elaisse sighed.

"I was lucky to have found even a nag," Jonathan said.

Then he looked up at her, peering intently, as if once again deciding something. Suddenly he said, "Here, take one of your pounds back. The horse didn't cost me anything. I stole it."

"I figured you did," Elaisse said, and smiled as she was handed back a pound.

"Good luck to you," Jonathan said.

"Listen, would you want to come with me? You can ride behind me. He may be a nag, but you're little, and this horse can carry both of us."

Once more Jonathan hesitated, as if deciding again. Then he said, "No, you go on. I can't leave London. It's the Jews, you know. They are out there in the country now, poisoning wells out there. I think the Jews left London, though. Most people have, you know. One way or another, so many people have gone. But I want to stay because this is my home. It's all I know."

"If you're sure—" Elaisse hesitated, wondering if she should talk to him about the Jews, but then she simply smiled and said, "Yes, good luck to us both."

She mounted the horse and flicked the reins. She was going home.

And when she finally left London behind and reached the country, Elaisse realized that she had forgotten how wonderful the world really was. The beauty of the English countryside astonished her. How could she have left this extraordinary place? The meadows were brown and soggy from the winter, but the open spaces revitalized her. Even though it was still very cold, the scent of a promised spring was in the air, and she breathed deeply.

Chapter Eight

In the tiny rural village of Grayton, miles from London, the doctor burned rosemary in his cook fire in order to fill his cottage with pleasant-smelling smoke.

He had worn his protective mask for weeks, rarely taking it off, even though he no longer saw patients. He refilled the bird-like beak daily with dried flowers because there were none fresh this time of year. Straps held the mask to his face. The mask had glass openings for the eyes and a curved beak shaped like a bird's. Two small nose holes in the beak allowed air to be filtered through aromatic items packed within.

He placed more dried flowers and sweet-smelling lavender throughout the cottage, including upon the floor where so many herbs were strewn over the dirt hardpan that they reached three inches high.

I mustn't allow any bad air to reach me, he thought. *Everything must be sweet to combat the foulness of invisible devils.*

The only time he took the mask off was to drink a mixture of apple syrup, rose water, and mint to sweeten his deep abdominal workings, just in case the bad air had penetrated inside.

He bled himself frequently these past few weeks, always careful to look closely at the deep red fluid for signs of sick blood or scum that rose to the surface, signifying that toxins had entered his body. He knew that blood could carry poisons, so by releasing it out of his body, he would be removing those poisons from his system.

The doctor bled himself out of different veins at key points in his body: the neck to cleanse his brain, the armpit to cleanse his liver, and the inside elbow of the left arm to cleanse his heart. But instead of making him feel stronger, the constant bleeding left him feeling weak and fatigued. Furthermore, on this day he felt too warm, even though it was the dead of winter outside.

He reached for his sharp scalpel; it was time to cleanse his liver. Perhaps that would relieve the feeling of sluggishness he was experiencing.

The doctor pulled his shirt away from his chest and groped under his armpit to search for the vein.

He felt a lump growing there.

He was doomed.

The doctor froze for a moment, then became resigned to his fate. He had seen too many of his patients with the same symptoms than to try to fool himself that it could be anything else but the pestilence.

He finally took off his beak-mask, and it tumbled out of his grasp to the floor. He decided he would lie down to await his death.

As the doctor lay on his bed growing sicker and sicker, a branch of burning rosemary fell out of the cook fire onto the layer of dried herbs on the floor. Within minutes, the whole cottage was engulfed in flames.

Late February 1349

She had to ride slowly, because the nag wouldn't gallop no matter how many times she kicked his sides.

But he did trot, and the farther away from London Elaisse rode, the more she was aware of the changes in the degrees of cleanliness. She left the dirt and filth of the city streets behind, and was eager to embrace the freshness of the country air, which seemed so pure because of the recent rains.

She had learned more during her brief stay in London than in her entire lifetime. Maybe someday she would be glad she had gained this experience. But today was not that day.

All day she rode, with only a short break for lunch. She found a cold, clear stream and drank deeply and then chewed her mutton jerky. Because she had passed many streams that were swollen from the rains, Elaisse was not concerned about lack of water.

It was dark when she reached the town of Grayton. Stopping her tired old horse, she sniffed the air. It smelled like there had been a very recent fire somewhere nearby. She hoped someone in the tiny village would take her in for the night so she wouldn't have to sleep outdoors. It was, after all, February and that meant it was very cold.

Suddenly she heard someone approaching from behind her. A horse was galloping towards her from the direction of London at a very fast pace.

Elaisse snapped the reins and the old, tired horse tried to bolt forward, but instead he stumbled and fell. She fell with him, tumbling out of the saddle and landing very hard on the wet, muddy ground; then she purposely rolled to get out of the way of the horse's falling body.

The horse lay prone on the soggy, cold ground. She pushed him but he didn't move. Was he dead? There was no time to make sure. She only knew that the old nag, if still alive, didn't appear that he would be getting back to his feet any time soon.

She started running towards the village, knowing that she couldn't wait for the horse. She could hear the stranger getting closer and closer. Whoever it was, he was pushing his horse to its limit in speed.

Elaisse ran up to the first cottage in the village and frantically knocked on the door. When no one answered, she pushed it but it was stuck shut. She glanced over her shoulder. She could see the man now. He was close enough to be within her view, but in the darkness, he appeared only as a form on a horse.

She ran to the next cottage, and this time didn't bother to knock. She shoved the front door and it opened inward. She rushed inside the dark cottage and slammed the door behind her, gasping for breath.

She could hear the man through the door as he reined his horse to a stop in front of the cottage and dismounted.

He was coming for her.

Elaisse ran away from the door, and quickly searched for a place to hide. She came across a bed at the back of the room, and nearly gagged.

Lying on the bed was a corpse, rotted with time. The skin was slipping off the skull, and the hands were long bones that stretched out from the sleeves. The clothes were sinking into the torso as the body disintegrated. It was impossible to tell if it had once been a man or a woman. The dead person must have been lying there a long, long time.

Elaisse whirled around and faced the door. She knew she didn't have the time to be distracted by the dead body on the bed. She dug in her satchel and pulled out her long, shiny knife. As she had done once before, she held it with both hands at head level, ready to thrust.

Suddenly the stranger was pounding on the door.

"Go away!" Elaisse cried out. "I have a weapon and I intend to use it!"

The man called her name through the door, and she froze with surprise.

She threw her knife down and pulled open the door. "Roger!" she exclaimed. "How dare you chase me down like some sort of common criminal!"

He laughed, entering the cottage. "Common criminal? Isn't that what you expect from me anyway?"

"Oh, nothing about you has changed!" Elaisse said, forgetting that just a few moments ago, she had been so very frightened. "How did you find me?"

"I looked for you at the Taylor store, but nobody seemed to be living there anymore. I went up and down your street looking for anyone who may have seen you. There are not a lot of well people in London any more, are there?"

"No there aren't," she said. "But go on, how did you find

me?"

"I ran across a fishmonger named Edmund who had just seen you. So, I figured you had left for your castle, but I knew you couldn't have gotten very far in such a short time. By the way, did you know that Edmund tried to sell me three dried fish for a pound? Who on earth would be stupid enough to pay those prices?"

Elaisse reddened. "Why, no one would."

Roger fell silent, studying her. Then he asked, "Aren't you the least bit glad to see me?"

That was all she needed. Elaisse fell into his arms, and hugged him tightly. They were both very glad to see each other. Together, they reminded each other of a simpler, happier time, one that was free of disease and death.

And then she broke away from his embrace. "We need to leave this cottage," she said. "There's a dead body in here."

Roger laughed, inciting her anger.

"There's nothing funny!" she snapped.

"I'm sorry," he said, trying to control his laughter. "It's just that you have such a strong reaction over one dead body. After all the dead people you must have seen in London over the past two months, you shouldn't be so surprised to see one more."

"I don't care what you say. I won't share a cottage with a diseased body."

"All right," Roger said, "we'll leave this cottage. But I want to look for another one that's empty. There have been so many abandoned villages lately that I haven't had to sleep outside for a long time."

"It's so sad," Elaisse said, "all this sickness and death."

"Yes, and it could be us joining the dead any day now," Roger said, then seeing her expression, he added, "That's all the more reason why we should live for the moment. I figure you're heading back to Wynham Castle. But now that I've had the good fortune to find you before you reached home, I'd like to talk you into staying here in Grayton for a while."

He took her hands in his own, then continued, "Stay with me,

Elaisse. Let's enjoy each other while we can—let's savor our flesh while it's still whole. I came to find you because I've been thinking of you. Let's find an empty cottage and spend the night together, savoring each other's warmth."

She figured he was cajoling her. "We're not man and wife, so we can't sleep together in the same cottage."

He frowned. "The world has changed, so the rules have changed."

She sighed. "Yes, I suppose the world *has* changed. It's gotten to the point that every day, I wonder if it is to be my last."

"All the more reason for us to be together while we still can."

"I have to admit," she said, "that I'm very glad to see you. I've felt so alone."

She took his hand, and he led her out the cottage door. They tried the cottage next door, and found it empty. It looked as though it had held a family at one time, because there were three beds in the corner. To guess how many people had lived in the cottage was impossible to do, as typical families often slept two or three siblings to a bed.

Roger went back outside to tie up his horse as Elaisse stepped inside the cottage. She sniffed the air of the deserted family home and determined that nothing smelled out of the ordinary. Because the cottage was dark, she could not see clearly as to what condition it had been left.

But when Roger stepped inside and stood next to her, he touched her and she knew that she wanted to be with him. She felt in her gut that the timing was right. For the first time in her life, she had no doubts about taking a lover.

Perhaps living among so many people who had died made her dwell in the present so much more. Perhaps she had realized that maybe the present was all she had. She was so happy to see Roger that the virginity she valued now seemed secondary. All she knew was that right now, in this moment, he had somehow found her, and she wanted to give herself to this man and to take what he could give her in return.

After witnessing so much death, she needed the presence of a living human being, one who could touch her, and one who could bring her a little happiness in a crazy, unhappy world. She learned that happiness could be fleeting, and she wanted to capture a moment of it, even if it were only a single moment. It would be her moment, hers and his.

So she told him that this house was just fine, and he led her to the largest bed in the corner, which was still very small. He lifted her chin and kissed her deeply and passionately. He began taking her hair out of the confining braids, and loosened her woolen cloak until it simply dropped upon the floor. He began removing her clothes, all the while still kissing her, and he murmured how beautiful she was.

I think I love him, Elaisse thought. *I know it's crazy because I really don't know him, but I swear I think I love him.*

She was so overwhelmed with feelings that she wasn't sure if she wanted to cry or to scream her happiness from the rooftops. She trembled in anticipation as he lowered her onto the bed. Closing her eyes, she gave in to her sentiment for this man. What was sexual for him was greatly emotional for her, and the tears quietly traveled down her cheeks.

Roger was unaware of the magnitude of her feelings, and only wanted her, and he told her truthfully that he had dreamed of this moment for many weeks. Now that his dreams were reality, he seemed to savor every moment, and he whispered that he was drinking in her flesh until he was drunk with her body.

Roger slowly entered her, gently probing the newness of the experience. He took his time and murmured soft words of appreciation and told her she was beautiful. She felt pain, but her desires soon overpowered any uncomfortable sensations, replacing them with hot stimulation that engulfed her whole being. She gasped at her longing, and Roger quickened the pace, loving her with fervor and excitement. She cried out at the finish and gripped him tightly with her arms.

He lay close to her when it was over, and she welcomed his presence. So this was what it was all about, to truly love another human being, not just with her mind, but with her body as well.

Roger held her, and whispered in her ear that she was special, and her heart thrilled at his words.

And afterwards she started to have doubts. Would he stay with her? There was once a point in her life when she wouldn't have cared, but now her feelings for Roger were growing quickly. She didn't want to lose him, but then she told herself, *I'll only think about this moment. Nothing will destroy this moment. I'll worry about tomorrow if I live to see it.*

Roger lay on his back and put one arm underneath her. With his other arm, he stroked her hair while she laid her head on his chest, listening to the pace of his heart gradually slow from the quick rhythm of a few moments before. After a long time, his grip loosened around her as he drifted off to sleep. Elaisse slept soon afterwards, and the night was still and sweet.

In the morning, she opened her eyes and was momentarily confused as to her surroundings, then she relaxed as she remembered. She looked at the cottage. It was small as was the fashion, but it seemed fairly clean. How many people had lived here, loved here, laughed here?

It was yet another thing she didn't want to think about. That was another lifetime, seemingly long ago. This new life was the only one she had now; the past didn't matter because it was gone and life would never mirror it again.

Roger awoke, and reached for her. They made love again, the brightness of the sunlight streaming through the cottage window, so that their glistening bodies were almost illuminated. For Elaisse, that morning was the happiest time she had ever known.

Afterwards, she told him she'd like to take a bath. Roger was incredulous. "A bath in times of sickness?" he exclaimed. "That would be the death of you for sure!"

"No, no," she said, "let me tell you some of the things I learned in London. Baths aren't dangerous. I took a lot of them in London, and I'd always felt better afterwards. I've discovered that things I've been told all my life are simply not true. Like opening windows! Not all air is bad; I've found that fresh air can cure nausea. And nobody was able to bleed me all through the

Great Dying in London, and yet, I was never stricken with the pestilence."

Roger seemed skeptical, and it showed in his face.

Elaisse frowned. "You were the one who told me that I needed to think for myself."

He burst into laughter. "And so you are! Now, let me see you smile again. You can take your bath if you can find a washtub, and believe me, I'll be delighted to watch you. Of course, you'll have to boil the water first since it's so cold out this time of year."

She looked around the cottage, and something occurred to her. "You know what? There are no rats around here."

"How would you know that?"

"Because the kitchen is so clean," she observed. "Take a look around. Where are the rodent droppings? All cottages have rodent droppings around the cooking area, except for this one. I wonder why."

"Well," he said, still lying on the bed, "maybe most of the rats died from the pestilence. I've seen all sorts of animals die, not just people. Except for horses; for some reason, they seem to be lucky."

"You could be right," Elaisse said. "Anyway, I never want to see another rat for as long as I live."

"And let's hope we both live long enough to keep enjoying each other here in Grayton!" Roger smiled. "But for right now, I'm hungry. Let's say we get up and find breakfast? I'll hunt for rabbit or grouse, and while I'm doing that, why don't you go to the fields and dig up turnips?"

She thought, *Of course! Why should we suffer with mutton jerky when fresh food could be obtained?*

She decided right then and there that she would indeed stay in Grayton with Roger. He had an answer for everything, and after all she had been through, she was relieved to let someone else take the lead and make decisions for a change. Before, in London, she had been forced by fate to lead the way not only for herself, but for Thomas Taylor as well. Now she only wanted to rest and recuperate from all the emotional horror she had seen and experienced in London. With Roger, life seemed fresh and bright again.

She stepped out into the cold sunlight and got her first look at the tiny village that was once Grayton. She was amazed at how quickly she had adapted to the enormity of London. Grayton was such a drastic change from the big city that she had forgotten on what a small scale villages were built. Now she realized she must get accustomed once again to towns that were dwarfed in size compared to London.

She noticed that one of the cottages in Grayton had recently burned. So that was the scent of fire she had smelled the previous night. But events of late were out of the ordinary all over, and a fire was just another bad thing in the midst of so many bad things.

Elaisse sighed. Was she becoming calloused and hardened to life at its most wretched? But wasn't that a form of emotional self-protection; a barrier against madness?

She didn't know any answers. She had seen too much sorrow and trouble as of late and hadn't had a minute to slow down and internally process everything she had experienced. She needed time to review events and to mull the impact over in her mind.

She decided she would do that during her stay in Grayton. She would use this time, not only to enjoy Roger's company, but also to sort everything out and to find out just how emotionally scarred she might have become because of the Great Dying.

And perhaps, during this time of recuperation, Elaisse could find a way to heal.

For now, she needed to concentrate on the present, so she went to a field behind a farmhouse. She took a trowel and a bucket, and began digging. The ground was frozen so her progress was slow. But finding enough turnips to make a stew was the reward for her efforts.

Maybe Roger would come back with fresh meat, and if so, what a meal they would have!

But Roger came back with more than just a slain rabbit.

Roger came back leading a new horse.

"Where did you find him?" cried Elaisse with joy. "All I had before was a nag, and he died when he got me here, poor thing."

"He was grazing out in a field. He still had a halter and lead on him," Roger said. "But we won't be needing your brand new horse for a while, will we? After all, we're not going anywhere. It's just you and me and a whole empty village now."

She felt her knees melt. She had heard that expression about melting knees, and now she knew what it meant. She looked at Roger and liked what she saw. He was tall, blonde, and rugged. His eyes were deep blue and his smile beautiful, and he was still young enough to have all his teeth. Dimples deeply etched his cheeks when he grinned, and suddenly she wanted to stay in Grayton forever.

She knew right then that she could never leave Roger. But he had left her before. Would he leave her again someday?

Elaisse forced herself to stop that line of thinking. *He's here today, and he'll be here tonight. I don't want to remember yesterday, and tomorrow might bring the pestilence. So I need to always only think of the present. And Roger is in the present.*

They ate fresh stew and made love by the warmth of the cook stove, which they kept burning to combat the cold February air. At about midnight they saw that it began to snow. Elated, they dressed warmly and frolicked in the snow like children, grabbing snowballs and throwing them at each other, and tasting snowflakes on their tongues.

The next morning it rained, washing away the snow. Elaisse and Roger lounged in the cottage together, eating leftover stew and experiencing endless fascination with each other's touch.

And so their days went. Roger was cheerful and showered Elaisse with great attention and caring affections. Elaisse was enormously happy. She was in love.

After a while, she began to convince herself that she and Roger would always live together in the solitary village of Grayton. She believed that London was over and Wynham Castle would never materialize.

It was only Grayton. It was only she and Roger, living and loving in Grayton.

But in March, Roger became restless.

Chapter Nine

Wynham Castle was unnaturally quiet, as most of the servants had refused to report to work, instead remaining fearfully within the village. The specter of illness and death stealthily prowled through the night, sneaking up on its victims and ensnaring them with lethal tentacles. The villagers were desperate, isolating themselves and trying all sorts of folklore remedies to ward off Satan's evil.

William, the Lord of Wynham Castle, did not want to change his routines. He was determined to maintain the appearance of normalcy. Whether he was deceiving himself or simply trying to prevent pandemonium was not clear to his wife. But one day, William wanted to ride, and a servant to deliver his horse could not be found.

William went into the stable himself to retrieve his mount. In the dim sunlight streaming between the stable wallboards, he could see that the horses had not been cared for, the stalls had not been mucked in days, and that infuriated him.

He noticed the dead body of a rat lying in the straw in one of the stalls. The fur on the rat was matted and was falling out in tufts from its body. Its eyes had sunken into its skull. But what turned Williams' stomach were the squirming, crawling maggots that ravaged the rat's flesh, entering and exiting the hide as they devoured everything in their paths. Beetles and ants traveled in procession across the body, some eating the rat, others eating the maggots that ate the rat.

He had seen so many dead rats lately. At first, William had simply ordered the servants to dispose of the bodies, but now the servants were few and William was certainly not going to remove dead rats himself. So the rats simply decomposed where they died.

William didn't know that fleas can live in empty rats' nests for weeks without their hosts. The heat of the many horses in the stable created an ecosystem that warmed the temperature of the building, helping the fleas to survive without the rats.

But the fleas were hungry.

The fleas could detect a warm host coming within their range. Although their preferred hosts were rats, they could not afford to be choosy at this stage.

With frenzied energy, the fleas swarmed the ankles of the human in the stable. Their piercing and sucking mouthparts contained sharp, sword-like mandibles.

Many of these fleas had feeding blockages caused by *Yersinia pestis*, so they were unable to swallow the blood they so frantically sought.

In desperation, the fleas bit their new host again and again and again.

At the castle

Times of crisis often brought families together, and the noble family at Wynham Castle was no exception. Henry Sheffield rode quickly past the same castle gate through which his sister had run away just months before.

At nineteen, Henry was tall and thin, with the same golden hair and large, blue-gray eyes as those of his sister Elaisse. He had been away at school since he was seven, only visiting the castle on holidays. More recently, Henry had been away receiving military training.

Now he had come home.

Henry had decided that this time, he was home to stay.

He saw that his horse dripped with sweat and foamed at the flanks because he had ridden his mount very hard. But he felt justified to ruin the horse because speed was of the essence.

He had rushed home, having gotten word that his father was

very sick.

Could his father be ill of the pestilence?

Thoughts raced through his mind. On one hand, Henry respected and cared for his father, even though he had lived away from home the majority of his years since he had been seven. On the other hand, Henry felt a thrill of excitement with the idea that if his father were to die, he would become Lord of Wynham Castle. Providing he could find a way to put a halt to the rights of his mother, of course.

Henry jumped off his horse and threw down the reins, expecting a servant to care for the animal. When no servant materialized, Henry simply let the horse go loose. He knew that his mount wouldn't go very far with its reins dangling to the ground, and besides, the horse was ruined anyway, so its fate did not concern him.

The main door to the keep was operated from inside by chains and pulleys. The guard recognized Henry and allowed him to enter the castle. Henry ignored the guard as he ran past. It was, after all, not Henry's habit to acknowledge the working class.

Henry climbed the steep stone stairs, noticing that it was very damp and also very cold in the stairwell. He slowed his pace as he climbed; the stairs were wet and slippery. When he reached the third story, Henry made his way through the dimly lit passageway.

Candles were made of melted animal fat and were impaled upon iron spikes mounted to the walls. The spikes had iron cups underneath to catch the dripping tallow. Because animal fat was used, the soot from the candles darkened the passageway walls. Henry quickly traveled down the hallway to his father's bedchamber, commonly called a solar.

He burst through the door. The bedroom was spacious and warmed by the burning fireplace in one of the walls. However, the room seemed almost dwarfed by the huge oak canopy bed in the middle. Unlike the commoners' sleeping mattresses, William's bed was padded by feathers throughout and covered with the finest linen and the warmest quilts. Interlaced ropes were tied to the heavy bed frame.

Henry came to the bedside and looked at his father. The older man had large, suppurating ulcers that ranged in color from blue to black. The disease had spread throughout William's lymph nodes.

His father seemed smaller than Henry remembered. Certainly he was thinner.

Even though he could see for himself, Henry asked his mother, "How is he?"

The Lady Hildred was holding her husband's hand. "Better," she said.

Henry looked at his mother oddly. "Is that so?"

"Before, he was confused, jerking with spasms, and had much delirium," Hildred told her son. "But see now how peaceful he is. He must be getting better."

Henry felt annoyed at his mother's naïveté, but did not express his thoughts. His opinion was that both of his parents had always tended towards tunnel vision; to only see within the limits of their expectations. He, on the other hand, felt he was young and worldly and therefore superior.

Whether his own important opinion of himself was right or wrong, Henry had witnessed so many victims of the pestilence that he recognized the truth about his father. Out of all those affected, only a minute number survived. Of all the many hundreds of diseased people he had seen, he could count the survivors on a single hand.

Now, looking at his father, Henry was certain that his father was going to die, and probably very soon. What Hildred had interpreted as resting peacefully, Henry recognized as coma.

William's buboes were swelled to almost bursting and the stench emitted from his body was overwhelming. Sores and open pustules oozed and wept. His skin color was pasty white, creating a contrast with the dark blotches, an indication of internal bleeding.

Henry pulled up a heavy oak chair and sat down. He joined his mother in a deathwatch. Time seemed to drag as they waited.

Sitting in the chair, Henry realized that he must have dozed off because he was suddenly awakened by his mother's scream. He jerked awake and told her to calm herself.

She pointed to his father, and Henry could see that William had died. The buboes had burst, and the putrid bodily fluids were leaking out upon the bed. The fetid odor fouled the room, and Henry lifted a kerchief to his nose in disgust.

"Call a servant," Henry commanded.

"There aren't any," Hildred said. "We're lucky we still have the guards."

"Then summon a guard!" Henry screamed at her.

He was used to commanding a military environment, and he felt pleasure when Hildred cowered beneath his orders. He took a grim satisfaction at the way his mother raced to obey him. She may have been his mother, but Henry barely knew her and felt no bond.

When the guard arrived, he came alone. Hildred was not with him. Henry instructed the man to take the body of his father outside to the fire pit to be burned. There was to be no burial because Henry did not want the castle grounds to be contaminated with the filth of the pestilence.

Finished with his father's remains, Henry went to the dining hall for wine and food. He had plans to make.

March 1349

Elaisse was living with Roger in Grayton. She was happy to be experiencing each day as it happened, with no thought of her past, and no thought of her future.

Her days were all the same, with no surprises. Everything flowed on an even keel, and she was grateful for the respite from her fear and her sadness. Life was good and she finally felt she had some serenity.

But were things really as calm as they seemed?

As February transitioned into March, she began noticing a subtle change in Roger. When March had been on the calendar for a couple of weeks, the changes in Roger became more pronounced.

Sometimes he seemed distracted, and she had to say his name more than once to get his attention. He began taking walks without her through the countryside. Other times he seemed to be thinking deeply, and would not share his thoughts. She fretted when Roger drifted away from her.

Conversely, there were still times when Roger was just the same as the man she had grown to love. He held her tightly at night and whispered into her ear about how he was glad she was in his arms. During the day, he seemed to enjoy hunting and appeared amused when she made a fuss over his kills. He sometimes helped her cook their meals, even though it was not something men would typically do. He even still held her hand when they walked through Grayton together as they searched other cottages for things they needed. Elaisse enjoyed Roger's company and the two of them laughed often.

Those were the good times.

But at other times …

They had never moved out of the first cottage they had slept in; they considered it their 'home cottage' even though they explored the others and took what they felt they needed form the other buildings. After experiencing so much calamity and upset in her recent life, Elaisse welcomed a sense of routine. She would worry on the days when Roger seemed so distracted.

On this particular morning in March, Elaisse woke before Roger, which was her custom. She snuggled close to him, loving his warmth. Loving him—wasn't that what she was doing? She considered her situation. Perhaps Roger didn't know that she cared so much for him.

Perhaps if she told him, he would stop thinking about leaving her.

Because Elaisse sensed that leaving her was exactly what Roger was thinking.

She contemplated the man who lay next to her, deep in sleep. She really knew very little about him, other than the fact that he had admitted his first name was Roger. She didn't know his last name or where he had come from. She didn't know what he did for a living besides what he had done for her, and she had no idea what other illegal activities he had done in his previous life.

But she knew he was handsome and he was intelligent. She knew that he thought as an individualist and not as an ineffectual conformist. She knew he had warmth and humor. She was beginning to learn his habits and his idiosyncrasies, and loved them both. She knew his faults, and accepted them. Most of all, she knew that when he made love to her, everything became right with the world.

But who was he? Did she really know Roger?

As she lay beside him, she looked at him with fondness, and touched his hair. She would find a way to keep him. She would bring him back to her from his distractions. She would make him want to stay in Grayton with her forever.

But how?

When he awoke, she hugged him fiercely. And then she did something that women just didn't do: she initiated the lovemaking. She brought the passion to a high level of excitement, then suddenly she cried out, "Stay with me forever!"

She felt his shoulders jerk away and tighten but he continued the lovemaking until he was spent. He lay back on the bed, and didn't reach for her like he usually did after their love.

"We have to talk," he told her.

She knew what that meant. She felt apprehensive, and was suddenly tempted to get out of bed and run away, yet at the same time, she wanted to stay and learn the truth. Was this the moment when he was going to tell her goodbye?

"I'm not the man you think I am," he said.

She sat up. "I don't care! I love you, just as you are!"

There. She had said it.

He rose on an elbow and looked at her. "I'm not in your social class."

Elaisse stared at him in disbelief. Of all the things she had expected him to say, that wouldn't have been it. Had she heard him correctly?

"What does social class matter anymore?" she asked him. "You've seen the pestilence strike both the rich and the poor. The Great Dying has been the end of the world as we knew it. Everything is different now. Everything!"

"Elaisse," Roger spoke softly. "You've been through so much that I can understand how you could mistake the good times we've had here in Grayton as love. But not everything in the world is different. Some things are still not right with society; there is still a need for change."

"Society! What are you talking about?"

"I'm talking about justice in the world."

"The world!" she screamed. "The world is dead! I'm talking about you and me!"

"Listen to me," he said. "When I told you I care for you, I do. But I've got things to do, and I've put them off for too long."

She couldn't speak. She was so completely stunned that she sat as though frozen. Here it was—he was going to leave her. The happy times in Grayton were about to end.

"The time we've spent together has really been wonderful," Roger went on. "The trouble is, I didn't mean for it to continue so long. I should have left sooner. Now it's hard to leave; hard for both of us."

Elaisse's shock turned to anger as she realized that this was his idea of an explanation. "Oh!" she cried. "So that's it? You think you can lay with me at night, then just walk away in the light of day? You think you can just discard me like a child does when he gets tired of a toy? You're the one who convinced me to stay here in the first place! If it weren't for you, I would be home right now."

He reached for her, but she jerked forcefully out of his grasp. Undaunted, Roger said, "I take full responsibility for asking you to stay, and I'm sorry. I care about you a lot; you're not a toy to me. You're a very wonderful woman. And I admire your spirit! But I've known for a couple of weeks now that I've been here in Grayton too long. I have to move on. I have something politically important that I have to do, and I can't drag you into it. If I stayed here any longer, I'd become miserable because I wouldn't be able to do what needs to be done to correct the wrongs of the world. And then I'd make you miserable. I never want to make *you* miserable."

Elaisse moved stiffly to the edge of the bed. "You think this is not making me miserable? And how can anything political be so important? Nothing political can possibly be as important as love!"

"I'm sorry if I'm hurting you," he said. "I would rather stab myself in the heart than to hurt you. But I told you I have something important to do and it's time to go. It's been said that the needs of the masses outweigh the needs of the few."

Elaisse angrily got out of bed, pulled off her nightdress, and threw it on the floor. Naked, she reached for her day clothes. "There are no more masses, so your argument has no value." Then she added, "I'm getting dressed. I have to travel today. You're not the only one who is leaving."

Roger tried to soothe her. "Think about what you are saying. Don't act irrationally. I know you want to go back to Wynham Castle. But you need an escort. At the very least, let me be your escort."

"No!" she shouted, pulling on her dress. "I'm perfectly capable of taking care of myself! I took care of myself just fine in London when you left me the first time. You've done your damage, and you're nothing but the common criminal I originally thought you were!"

Roger laughed. "I admire your bravery. Listen, you may think that everyone's dead, but they're not. There are still masses, including bad people out on the roads. You have more to learn."

"I've just learned one more lesson in life, haven't I?"

"And what's that?"

"Not to trust *you.* I'd be better off with the bad people on the roads instead of *you.*"

He winced a bit at that, then said, "Listen, let me take you back to Wynham. I owe it to you."

"We owe each other nothing. I've already paid the price for this lesson by the pain I feel. And now I hate you, so don't continue your arrogant speeches."

Fully dressed now, Elaisse stomped out of the cottage.

Roger quickly threw on his clothes and followed her outside. But no amount of persuasion could convince her to allow him to travel with her. Reluctantly, Roger helped her pack her saddlebag with enough supplies to see her through her journey.

And once on her horse, Elaisse knew that Roger was standing in the middle of Grayton's main road, watching her go, but she wouldn't turn her head to look back at him.

Hours later, she was getting used to her new horse on the road. He was smaller than her last mount but much more spirited. She felt grateful that she wasn't riding the nag that the street urchin had stolen for her in London.

She was surprised at how little she grieved over Roger during the first part of her journey, but then she realized that anger dispelled the pain of her loss. What a difference she had felt when she had lost John Wythe.

Poor John; she hadn't thought of him in so long. She was convinced that John would have come back to her if he had not been struck down in France, and how differently her life would have turned out had that happened.

She sobbed as she rode, but she didn't know if she cried for John or for Roger. She felt so empty, so hurt; and so very and completely alone.

And then suddenly she knew for whom she grieved. She absolutely knew.

She hated to admit it to herself, but it was for Roger for whom she was crying. She could barely remember John Wythe; it was as though he was a fictional character in a book because her memory of him had dimmed. She had never really known John except for a couple of superficial stolen moments in the stable.

But Roger had been a part of her daily life for over a month, and she had healed a great many emotional scars because of the happiness she had experienced with him. As she rode, Elaisse began to feel that her longing for Roger was almost a physical burden to carry, weighing her down.

She didn't want to miss him, so her thoughts turned to Wynham Castle. Maybe she could find hope there. At least she would have her parents. Elaisse thought about how good it would feel to see her mother and her father again, and also to see Fern, her maid. Part of her was apprehensive—would her father forgive her for running away? She had to take that chance. She wanted, absolutely *needed*, to go home.

She felt thirsty, and she could hear a stream up ahead. Picking her way through shrubbery, she guided her horse towards the sound of running water. She stopped at the clear stream, watered her horse, and drank deeply herself.

Then she lifted her head quickly because she thought she heard hoofbeats. Straining to listen, she slowly retrieved the knife from her satchel.

A voice called to her, and Roger burst from the underbrush, grinning sheepishly as he reined his horse to a stop.

"You again!" she shouted. "For someone who wants to leave me so badly, you keep coming back!"

"I've been following you," he said. "I thought I'd give you some time to cool off. But then you left the road and I worried I'd lost you. So I figured I'd better make myself known before I truly did lose your trail. Put your knife away, I know you're hiding it behind your back."

"I ought to use it on you just for spite," Elaisse said. "Maybe that would be the only way I could be sure you wouldn't follow me again."

He laughed while he dismounted. Then he grew serious. "I can't let you travel alone. Things are crazy in the world right now. I keep telling you that there are people who are convinced that they don't have long to live, so they want to rob and rape in the meantime. There are no constables anymore to stop them and they know it. Even if you're mad at me, let me escort you. Two people are safer than one in times of trouble. Let me take you back to Wynham."

As it would soon be dark, she was more open to his arguments. "I suppose you're right. But I am not going to share your sleeping blankets tonight, knowing you are just going to take off again as soon as we reach the castle."

Roger laughed, and Elaisse wondered why he always laughed at inappropriate times. It was exasperating.

"Well," he said, "I neither agree with you nor feel happy with your decision about wanting to keep me out of your bed tonight, but I'll respect your wishes. If I can't have your warmth later, then we'd better not sleep outside. Can you ride for another hour? There's another village up ahead."

They got back on their horses and rode together. The sunset was beautiful, and lifted her spirits. She didn't want to admit to herself how good it felt to have Roger at her side once again. But it did feel good, indeed.

They reached the village of Hobbs, which was slightly larger than Grayton. This village was not completely deserted. From a few of the cottages, Elaisse could see smoke coming out of the cook fire chimneys.

Roger approached an inhabited cottage and knocked on the door. It was the custom to welcome travelers for the night. But when a middle-aged man with unruly brown hair and the beginnings of a gray-flecked beard answered the knock, he demanded, "What do you want?"

"We're two travelers looking for a night's lodging," Roger explained.

The door slammed shut. Roger shrugged his shoulders and proceeded to the next cottage. While Elaisse waited on her horse, Roger knocked expectantly. When an old woman answered, he repeated his request.

The old woman practically snarled, "Sleep in the stable!" and Roger found himself with another door shut in his face.

"This is the rudest town I have ever seen!" Elaisse exclaimed.

"It's because they're so frightened," Roger said. "Fear makes people suspicious. People are trying to isolate themselves from the outside world. They don't know what causes the sickness and they're not taking any chances with strangers. Here, let's take that woman's advice and find the stables. Why don't you dismount so we can walk together?"

She swung down from the saddle, and they strolled together, leading their horses behind them. But when they reached the Hobbs' community stable, a dead rat lay at the door.

Repulsed, Elaisse said, "I'm not going in there."

"What?" Roger was surprised. "It's only a dead rat. It's one of hundreds. You can't tell me, after all you've seen, that you're afraid of a dead rat?"

"I've seen rats all over London," she told him, "and they were everywhere, in the houses and in the streets. And I saw horrible things that were done to two dead people in London when rats chose to nibble on their faces. You told me I'd get used to rats in London. Well I didn't!"

"Now Elaisse," he tried to persuade, "think about it. It's March, and maybe the days are warming up, but the nights are still very, very cold."

"No more rats."

Roger tied his horse to a wooden post, then started walking away.

"Where are you going?"

"To seek another cottage. Maybe I can find an empty one."

"Wait for me!" Elaisse said as she quickly tied her mount to the same post.

They knocked on first door they came across that had no chimney smoke. No one answered. Roger pushed the door and it opened. The cottage smelled musty and unused.

Roger went to the cook stove and started a fire. Elaisse rummaged around for a pot to stew some turnips that she had carried in her saddle bag. She threw some dried rabbit meat in the stew that would soften in the boiling water and in turn, flavor the mixture. Elaisse smiled to herself as she realized just how competent she had become in living off the land.

After they ate, Elaisse chose a bed. She threw her woolen cloak over the top of the bed for use as a blanket. She didn't bother to change into her night clothes but instead simply got under her cloak still wearing her day clothes. She could feel Roger's eyes upon her.

"No," she said simply, and turned over in the bed to face the wall.

Chapter Ten

As the death toll mounted across England, there were spiritual casualties as well.

Christian virtues such as piety, devotion, and selflessness were no longer accepted as unfailing methods to achieve God's favor. Instead, superstition ran rampant as people tried to find explanations or justifications for the tremendous loss of life.

Some people were convinced that sailors brought the pestilence to England, since the disease seemed to begin at the coastlines. Therefore, these people began to eschew eating fish, in the belief that the seawater was contaminated. No spices were used, since most spices were brought to England by ship from faraway places.

Most people agreed amongst themselves that the primary cause of the Great Dying was bad air. People sought out low spots in the land that were sheltered from any wind. Windows were covered to prevent drafts. When not in use for meal preparation, the cook stoves were to be used to burn rosemary and other strong-smelling herbs.

People moved slowly in order not to exert themselves. Exertion meant heavier and deeper breathing and then more bad air could be sucked into the lungs. When sleeping, they considered it ideal to lie on their sides and not on their backs. Lying on their backs would point their noses skyward, and since everyone knew that bad air was heavier than good, the bad air would simply just fall into their nostrils if they slept on their backs.

Blood-letting was a common practice as a medical treatment for the illness. Not only surgeons and doctors did this, but barbers as well. Instruments were not cleaned but simply wiped off between patients, and hands were never washed, as nobody had any concept of germs. If a patient fainted from blood loss, the practice was to simply pour cold water on the face and then to continue the bleeding.

One of the most common manners in which to deal with the pestilence was to flee. Husbands left wives, mothers left children, and siblings left siblings. But as March turned to April, there became less and less uninfected places towards which to run.

Early April 1349

Roger rode beside her as they reached the main gate of the Wynham Castle grounds. He reined his horse to a stop.

"This is as far as I can go," he told her.

"I suppose I should say thank you for being my escort," Elaisse said. She was experiencing so many mixed emotions. She was excited to be back home, but disheartened to be losing Roger yet another time.

She didn't want him to know how badly she wished he would stay. She figured she had already reduced herself previously to a fool's level when she had begged him to stay in Grayton with her. Now she was determined that she would let him ride away without complaint, no matter how badly it hurt her to do so.

"Elaisse—" Roger began.

She refused to look at him. She simply waited for the guard to open the gate.

"Elaisse," he tried again, "could I come back to see you sometime?"

She turned to him in fury. "How dare you continue to treat me like a toy that you can pick up and then discard on a whim!"

"I guess that means no. I've always admired your spirit, Elaisse. You're not a little girl anymore; you've become quite a woman." He grinned, yet the smile didn't reach his eyes. "Goodbye, Elaisse. You're certainly someone who I'll never forget."

He turned his horse and rode off. And he was gone…again.

The guard finally opened the gate.

She had forgotten how wonderful it could feel to be home. The beauty of the Wynham Castle grounds astonished her. How could she have left this extraordinary place? The meadows were brown and soggy from the ending winter, but the open spaces revitalized her. The cheerful early forsythia was in bloom with yellow brilliance, and the crabapples were showing signs of rejuvenation as buds swelled upon the branches. The scent of a promised spring was in the air, and Elaisse breathed deeply.

But…something was missing. Where were the people?

She asked the guard who opened the gate, "Where are the gardeners? Or the servants? Or the other guards?"

The guard looked at her strangely. He spoke three words. "The Great Dying."

Elaisse was devastated. "Here too?"

"Everywhere."

They reached the main door and she dismounted and gave the guard her horse. She ran inside, too energized and hopeful to move slowly, bad air or not.

She rushed through the castle, searching for her parents. She felt a dawning that most of the castle was empty of people. She felt the first undertone of fear—where were her parents?

She refused to let the thoughts in the back of her mind come forward. Her mother had always been a fixture in the castle, albeit a silent one, and her father had always seemed larger than life. There was no possible way that the pestilence could have touched either of her parents. It couldn't be possible!

She entered the great hall. She sucked in her breath with surprise when she saw her brother seated at the table.

He was dressed in a tan tunic and matching leggings. His shoes were of the highest quality, with the toes long and pointed as was the latest fashion. His golden hair was almost as long as her own, and almost as thick. Elaisse barely recognized her own brother, for he was beginning to show the maturity of a man, not the child she had last seen, seemingly so long ago.

"Henry!" Elaisse cried. "What are you doing here?"

"Is that supposed to be a greeting?" Henry asked.

She realized that his tendencies towards sarcasm had not mellowed over the years. He lifted a silver goblet to his lips, and Elaisse noticed a flask of wine on the table.

She sat across from him at the table. "No, of course not; I'm sorry to have sounded so abrupt. I was just surprised to see you, is all. I didn't know you were through with your military employment."

"I'm not through with military employment. Military employment is though with me. Haven't you heard the news? The war with France is at an impasse. It seems there are no longer enough men on either side to do battle."

"Well," she said, "at least that's one good thing to come out of all of this. It stopped the war."

Henry stared at her. "Are you daft?"

"Oh, I don't know, maybe I am. I'm just so tired of bad news. Where's Daddy?"

"Dead." Henry lifted the goblet to his lips again. "The pestilence killed him a week ago."

Elaisse blanched. She was quiet for a moment, trying to absorb the impact of his news. The nagging fear that had lain at the back of her mind came forward. Somehow she had known. "And Mother?"

"Alive. She's upstairs in her solar," he told her, "but now she's even more daft than you are."

Elaisse ignored the rude comment, not knowing who he was insulting more, she or their mother. Instead, she asked, "Where is Daddy buried? I want to go to his grave and pay my respects."

Henry laughed sourly. "Buried! There's to be none of that. Everyone who dies is to be burned, not buried."

She couldn't believe her ears. "You've burned our father? Do you realize what you've done? And who put you in charge of these decisions, anyway?"

"I put myself in charge, and you'd better obey me just like everyone else does. I need to dispose of dead bodies quickly. You obviously haven't seen the village lately. There are no places left for any burials. And I won't have the castle grounds contaminated with death." He took a drink. "After all, I have to live here."

Elaisse was stunned. "I didn't know the pestilence had made its way to Wynham. Somehow I had hoped that Wynham would be spared, but I see now that was a dreamer's folly."

She was quiet a moment, then added, "I'll help you with the villagers. We should see to their needs."

"You won't help me with anything," Henry said, his voice dripping with venom. "I've already told you that I'm in charge at Wynham Castle. I make all the decisions around here. And I make those decisions alone."

"You're drunk," Elaisse accused.

"Not quite, but I'm quickly getting there," Henry said. He refilled his goblet with unsteady hands.

She couldn't take another moment of it. She jumped up, and her chair fell to the floor behind her. She ran out of the room to the castle keep. The stairs seemed darker than she remembered, and she noticed that not all of the candles in the passageway were lit.

The world as I once knew it has ended. Even here at Wynham, it is all gone, Elaisse thought.

On the third floor, she found her mother in the main bedroom solar. Hildred was sitting in front of a vanity mirror, brushing the hair that was streaked with many strands of gray. For a moment, she had a fleeting memory of another time when she herself had brushed her hair in front of a mirror, getting ready to attend a jousting tournament. What a lifetime ago that was!

At the sound her daughter made, Hildred turned around. "Elaisse!" the older woman exclaimed, and instantly Elaisse knew she was forgiven for running away. Hildred said, "I'm so glad to see you! I had hope against hope that you would somehow survive the pestilence!"

Elaisse ran to her mother, and the two embraced tightly. "I'm sorry I ran away! I didn't want to hurt you or Daddy. I just couldn't marry Sir Geoffrey. I wasn't planning to be gone for very long, just until Geoffrey found another wife. But the fate of the world turned very bad, didn't it?"

They continued to hold each other very tightly, quietly celebrating the idea that they had each discovered the other still alive. They remained together for a while, both giving silent prayers of gratitude.

Finally they separated and looked at each other. Hildred said, "I worried about you every minute of every day. But of course you realize it wasn't *me* who insisted that you marry Sir Geoffrey Gladden."

Elaisse pulled up a chair and sat next to her mother. She told Hildred all about her apprenticeship with Thomas Taylor, but she omitted any details about the sickness and death she had witnessed in London. It was already understood how terrible the pestilence was; there was no need to bring it to the forefront.

Finally she told her mother, "I'm sorry about Daddy."

"It's a shame he had to die the way he did," acknowledged Hildred, "but now I will finally be able to come out from under his restraints."

Elaisse stood up. "What?"

Hildred went on, "I never had any say in anything of consequence. It was always yes dear this and yes dear that."

Elaisse was speechless. She simply stood there, staring at her mother.

"Now Elaisse," Hildred said, noticing her daughter's anguish. "I know you loved your father. And he was good to you. But he was never good to me. So now you know how I really feel, which is relief that he died. I'll run Wynham Castle now from here on out. I've always had ideas about how to manage things, but your father never let me express my ideas. And now I don't need his permission."

"I need some rest," Elaisse said, and she turned to leave.

"Your room is exactly the same as how you left it," her mother called after her.

Elaisse didn't want to hear another word for fear she would

become sick. She quickly left her mother, but didn't go to her bedroom solar as her mother had suggested. Instead, she made her way to the castle's chapel. Since it was not a Sunday, there were no priests or bishops present, provided any had survived the pestilence anyway, which she didn't know. The chapel's emptiness made the large size of the room seem omnipotent. In the unoccupied space, sounds echoed.

Ornate religious symbols decorated the walls, and the chancel was spread with a colorful cloth complete with gilded edgings. Elaisse ignored the balcony and went to the floor seating instead, because she wanted to be as close to the chancel as possible. She sat on a stone pew and rested her head in her hands, elbows on her thighs.

She tried to find some sort of perspective on the events happening around her. She searched her memory for any psalms or parables that preached strength, but her mind came up blank. She looked into her soul to find her faith.

She now felt that God had not caused the pestilence as punishment for mankind. She had observed that the sickness took both the good and the bad, and also those who were in-between. Elaisse searched for her faith, trying to evaluate it.

She felt that God was perfect, but was His creation? The soul was simply carried in a vase that was the body, and like a vase, the body could be broken. It was said that man was created in His image, but was merely appearing like God enough? While God had no earthly substance, the human body contained flesh that could age, flesh that could be punctured with wounds, and flesh that could be invaded by illness. God was not punishing the people; it was simply that the vessel carrying the soul was fragile.

Would she be able to maintain her faith through the fear and the abhorrence, through the shock and the horror, and through every other inconsolable emotion that one experienced from living among constant illness and death?

Elaisse decided that yes, she could maintain her faith.

Doing so came through an acceptance of death as a natural consequence of living. To try to see the world on a grand scale meant to view the human population as a collective, and not as individual elements.

It was like the stars in the sky: none were less beautiful because there were so many, but together the stars made for a brighter light.

She decided that she believed the human race would somehow survive, just not all of its members. This was not to say that each person was not important. It was to say that each person was not all-important to the grand design of the world.

She contemplated that having faith meant having trust, and having trust lessened her stress. *So that is the design of faith,* Elaisse mused.

Faith could keep a person sane when the world around him or her was insane. No reasonable person could possibly think that the world was only good or bad in continuing moderation. A reasonable person could understand that the world goes along its own path with its own directions and sometimes the good or the bad could turn extreme. A sane person had to learn to accept what could not be changed.

She suddenly understood that she could not control people, places, or things. She could only control her reaction to people, places, or things.

And so Elaisse felt that acceptance was the key. What else could she think? She had to give up the presumption that she could change the events happening around her by sheer force of will. She could not change the pestilence; that was an event of such a horrific magnitude that it was out of her reach. Instead, she had to break down the event into little bits and pieces to see what she *could* change.

What she could change was her attitude. She needed to be grateful for what she still had, and let go of what she had lost. She needed to stop coveting the past because that was useless, and stop fearing the future, because that was equally useless. She needed to stay in the present and make the most of it.

Elaisse got off her knees, and looked at the alter. She felt restored, and had a renewed purpose. In a crazy, sad world where there wasn't a lot to be thankful for, she would learn to be thankful for little things. Keeping her sanity was certainly something to be thankful for. It was a start.

Little bits and pieces, Elaisse thought, *the quilt of life is made from little bits and pieces sewn together.*

She left the chapel feeling calm and replenished. She understood that she was alive and well at this very moment, and this moment was all she had. It had to be enough, so it *was* enough.

She went back to the keep and climbed the dark stairs to her bedroom solar. When she went into her bedroom, it was just as Hildred had said. It was exactly the same as how she had left it.

She was hit with an intense wave of nostalgia. How could something remain so unchanged in a world that had become so changed?

But the room only contained objects. Of course objects could remain the same. It was people who were changeable.

I must stop my wishes for the past, Elaisse thought. *I can't bring back what was, and thinking about it will only distract me from what is.*

She lay on her canopy bed, and resolved that she would go to the village the very next day to see for herself how the peasants were faring during these harrowing times.

Chapter Eleven

To most, the Great Dying truly did seem like the end of the world, all over the Europe, first coming to Crimea in 1346 and then spreading rapidly along trade routes.

In Egypt, the deaths in Cairo mounted to over 300 per day. In the Mediterranean, populations were reduced between 40 to 50 percent. In Italy, Florence was estimated to have lost at least 20,000 inhabitants. Most of Europe's devastation averaged roughly 25 percent, but there were some towns that were said to have a death rate of 50 to 60 percent.

In Germany, there was a general breakdown of law enforcement and the cities were in shambles. In Holland, the draining and damming of wetlands came to a halt after a history of over 200 years of agricultural improvements. In Spain and other places, some villages were emptied altogether, eventually to become reclaimed by wilderness.

All told, between half to three-quarters of the entire world's population was to die.

The pestilence was thought to have arrived in England through the port of Melcomb Regis, in Dorset, sometime during the fall of 1348.

London was hit hard. England's largest city had around 50,000 people who were all crowded together in about the circumference of only a few square miles. The results were a devastatingly large death toll. London would not recover its pre-plague population until the mid-sixteenth century.

For much of Europe, the centuries-old way of life of serfs and lords crumbled because *Yersinia pestis* had removed the very foundations of the institutional way of life. Large numbers of both the upper and lower classes perished, so the old rules no longer accomplished the goals of socialism. A new individualism began to emerge.

Yet a great price was paid for this individualism. The price was the tremendous thinning of the populations of North Africa, the Middle East, Asia, and of course, Europe, where England lay.

Late April 1349

Elaisse woke early the next day, and left the castle before the sun rose. She chose to walk to the castle's village instead of riding, because she felt she had ridden so much as of late, and besides, the village was so close to the castle.

She wondered if Fern was still alive. She wanted to find out.

As she trekked down the main road that led to the village, she noticed that there was no one else traveling down the same road. In normal times there would be walkers, riders, wagons, and carriages. But on this day, she had the road all to herself, which was very unsettling.

She knew that the village was its own community, separate from the castle in terms of vocations and subsistence, but intertwined with the castle in terms of protection, contracts and leases. As she walked, Elaisse contemplated about how only the lord of the castle owned land, but villagers earned the rights to farm on that land by paying rents and by giving services. She was aware that the living standards of the peasants largely depended upon the limits, or lack of limits, that the lord of the castle charged for taxes. She wondered silently if this arrangement was just, or even moral.

Elaisse reached the first of the village cottages, but they seemed dark and deserted. She stood on the road for a moment, a little afraid to go further into the village, but needing to know what lay ahead.

The day was warm for April; the low clouds in the east made for a beautiful sunrise. The sun sat on the horizon like a fiery red ball, and the surrounding sky was lit with colorful pinks and oranges. *How could any devastation possibly occur in the midst of such a glorious morning?* she wondered. Still, the fact that the villagers were not going about their usual activities was an ominous sign.

Finally deciding to continue, she went to the door of the first cottage and knocked. The cottage looked lifeless. As she expected from the appearance of the house, there was no answer to her knock. She went to the next cottage and did the same. Again, no answer. But this time Elaisse pushed on the door to see if it would open. It did.

Cottages were very small, and usually contained only a main room. Peeking inside, in the dim light of the building, Elaisse could see the beds in the corner, and three or four benches. The cooking area contained a few iron pots but was otherwise empty.

Perhaps the past residents of this cottage had been well enough to flee, taking their necessary cookware with them. Elaisse knew that in normal times, any peasants who left the village could be found and punished for desertion, but these were not normal times, so it wouldn't surprise her if the occupants had simply run away.

Sighing, she left the cottage and stepped back outside. In the front yard, a chicken pecked the ground in its attempt to forge for food. In a corner of the yard by the road, a small dog lay unmoving, and Elaisse could see the dog's body undulating as a contrast of black beetles and white maggots moved freely through it. Whether the dog had died of the pestilence or had simply starved to death was not for her to know.

She moved on, passing by the next cottage because it was yet another one that appeared deserted. Elaisse walked quite a ways before she finally spied a home that had smoke rising from its cook fire chimney. She went to the door and knocked.

"No one can come in here!" a woman's voice shouted from inside. "There's sickness in this house!"

Startled, Elaisse backed away and left. She was heartened to see that the farther she walked towards the heart of the village, the more plentiful the occupied houses were starting to become.

She continued to the doorway of another cottage that had chimney smoke curling towards the sky from the roof.

She knocked on the front door, and heard activity coming from within. After what seemed to be a long while, a tired-looking man of about thirty came to the door. "What do you want?" he demanded in a loud, gruff voice.

"My name is Elaisse Sheffield," she said, "and I'm searching for someone, Fern Carver. She has red-brown hair and a mole on her cheek. She used to be a maid in our castle."

The man stared at her for a moment. "So, you're a Sheffield from the castle!" he suddenly shouted, scaring her. "You make us burn our own families when they die! What are you doing to help all of us who are losing our loved ones? What are you doing to find another doctor to replace the one who died? Or a priest? What are you doing about this pestilence? You are doing nothing! Nothing! So in return, I will do nothing for you."

The door loudly slammed shut, its sound reverberating down the lane.

Elaisse hesitated for a moment, too stunned to move. Then she recovered, and went to the next cottage to try again. When she knocked, no one answered even though she heard sounds coming from within.

She went to still another cottage. She knocked and was rewarded for her efforts when a small child answered the door.

"Hello," Elaisse greeted the little girl, "is your mother home?"

"She doesn't live here anymore," said the girl, who appeared to be around six, "because she lives with God now."

"How about your father?" Elaisse asked.

The little girl disappeared inside the house, and shortly an old, gray-haired man appeared at the door. "What do you want?" the old man asked, sounding impatient.

"Are you the girl's father?" Elaisse asked incredulously, as the advanced age of the man was apparent.

"No, of course not," snapped the man. "I'm her grandfather. Now, I repeat, what do you want?"

"I'm looking for Fern Carver—" Elaisse began, but was interrupted when the old man cut her off.

"Yes, yes, so, what about her?" the old man demanded, still impatient.

"Do you know her?"

"Of course I know her. All of us know everyone in this village."

"Can you tell me which cottage belongs to her family?" Elaisse asked.

The old man gave directions, then said he had to go back inside to see to his son, who would be meeting his Maker soon. Again, a door was slammed in her face. But this time she had gotten the information she needed first.

Elaisse quickly walked to Fern's cottage. She was overjoyed to see smoke coming from the cook fire chimney. She noticed that the front stoop had been freshly swept with a broom. Perhaps that meant that Fern had survived!

With high anticipation, Elaisse knocked on the cottage door. After a few minutes, Fern herself answered.

Both women stood staring at each other for a moment, then they broke the interlude by hugging. They began crying, but at the same time, they laughed through their tears. They separated from their embrace and began spurting words simultaneously, each saying almost the same thing at the same time. When they realized what they were doing, they both stopped speaking, and laughed again.

"I can't believe you're here!" Fern cried.

"I can't believe I've found you!" echoed Elaisse.

Suddenly Fern became somber, and she said, "I don't know if I should invite you inside or not. Most of my family has died. My brother is all I have left, and he's very sick. I stayed at the castle for a while after you left, but then I was summoned home to take care of my brother and sister after my parents died from the pestilence. Now my sister is also dead, and my brother soon will be as well, I'm afraid."

"Can I help?" Elaisse asked.

"You are of noble blood, so it is not your place to be a nurse. You are a lady of the castle," Fern said. "You cannot be near someone who has the sickness."

"The old rules no longer apply. The world is different today. I am a person just like you are now; just a person," Elaisse said. "I've seen victims of the pestilence everywhere I've been. I even nursed your uncle, Thomas Taylor, and for some reason I never caught the illness from him. That's why I don't think it's contagious. I don't know what causes the sickness, but I don't think you can get it by nursing sick people. So yes, I'll come inside and help you with your brother. And I'll tell you all about what happened to your uncle Thomas."

But when Elaisse entered the dimly lit cottage, the stench of sickness overwhelmed her. It told her that Fern's brother must be very bad indeed.

"Let's open the windows and let some air in here," Elaisse suggested.

"Oh no!" Fern protested. "We can't let the bad air get inside!"

Calmly Elaisse reasoned with Fern. She explained what she had learned in London when she had been nursing Thomas Taylor. "I felt so nauseous, and I was close to vomiting from the small of the sickbed. I opened a window because I was so desperate. But then the air from outside made me feel better. It stopped my nausea immediately. I'm telling you, Fern, that it's the truth. Maybe there *is* bad air in the world. But there is good air too. We need the good air right now."

Even though Elaisse had insisted she was "just a person," Fern was used to obeying her mistress, and so she agreed, although reluctantly. Elaisse pulled aside the curtains from both of the cottage windows. Instantly the cottage was transformed from a gloomy, dark hovel into a more cheerful, sunnier place. She opened both windows, and a fresh April breeze carried the smell of hyacinths inside. The windows were on the opposite sides of the room, so together they created a venting effect.

But from the otherwise quiet street, Elaisse could hear a wagon approaching. She cringed as she heard the familiar cry.

"Bring out your dead!"

Her face ashen, Elaisse turned to look at Fern. "Are there that many dying here that you need a push-cart to carry the bodies away?"

Fern nodded solemnly. "And we're no longer allowed to bury our families, either."

Elaisse just stared, knowing what Fern was about to say and dreading to hear it spoken aloud.

"The village had a messenger from the castle," Fern continued. "The messenger said that he was taking orders from your brother Henry. The messenger told the villagers that all of the dead must not be buried. They are to be burned."

Elaisse touched Fern's shoulder in sympathy. She didn't know what to say. After all, it was her brother Henry doing this.

Together they went to the sickbed to see to Fern's brother.

"His name is Edward," Fern said. "He was named in honor of our King Edward III. My poor brother Edward." Fern took a wet cloth and wiped his forehead.

It was very bad. Edward was in the last stages of the illness. He was comatose, and his pale skin was blotched with dark spots and there were pustules that drained from his face. His reddish-brown hair was plastered to his scalp with sweat. Elaisse could not see under the blanket, but she could imagine that Edward had large buboes under his arms that were probably swelled, engorged with blood.

"I'm so sorry," Elaisse said as she pulled up a chair and joined Fern at the bedside.

"At least he'll be at peace soon," Fern said. "It was worse with my sister. She had the *danse macabre*."

"Yes, I had seen some of that in London," Elaisse said. "It was a rare occurrence, though. I think the body goes awry. The *danse macabre*: the dance of death."

Fern agreed. "My sister Catherine couldn't control her movements. She went wild, jerking and dancing, before she became too sick to move any longer. In the village, it hasn't happened very often either, but on the rare occasion when a person is afflicted with the pestilence, they move in frantic spasms. The *danse macabre*."

Would the horror never end? Elaisse thought that the pestilence was very cruel indeed. Not only did it take away people's lives, but it also took away all possibilities of dying with peace and dignity.

Together the women sat at the deathbed, keeping watch and wiping Edward's forehead. But by three in the afternoon, Edward became very still and stopped breathing.

Fern moaned with her heartbreak. "He was all I had left."

Elaisse held Fern for a while, letting her grieve in her arms. Then she gently said, "I'll make a shroud."

Fern raised her head from Elaisse's shoulder. "But we have to give him to the push-cart man to be burned!"

"We'll give Edward a Christian burial."

"How?" Fern asked. "The churchyard was full a month ago. The priest himself has died. There is no way to give poor Edward a Christian burial, so now his soul is at risk. Poor Edward! He was only fourteen. But I suppose it is God's will."

"I don't think God caused this pestilence," Elaisse said.

Fern looked at her with a frightened expression.

Elaisse added, "God gets credit when things go right and when things don't go right, He is not blamed because it is simply 'God's will' and not for us to understand. I don't think it works like that." Then she paused, realizing her words should be comforting instead of lecturing. "I'm sorry, please forgive me, of course you are right."

Fern looked back at her brother, dead in his bed, and asked, "How will we save his soul?"

"He will not be burned. We'll secretly bury him in the kitchen garden behind the cottage, and no one will be the wiser. We will read prayers from the Bible for him. The Bishops gave laypeople the ability to have God's ear, so He will hear us. I never knew Edward, but since he was your brother, I'm sure he was a good boy. We will ask God to take Edward home."

"The kitchen garden has been planted so many times that now

the earth is soft and we can dig easily," Fern said. "This is early spring, and most gardens are being dug now. So yes, I think we can do this without anyone realizing. And Elaisse?"

Elaisse waited.

"I'm glad you're here to be with me in my time of need."

Shee smiled. "Fern, this is a new and changed world. You're not a servant any longer. You are my friend."

Fern sponge-washed Edward as Elaisse sewed a shroud from sheets. It was twilight when they were done. The women waited until it was fully dark, then they began digging in the night.

They dug for an hour in the dark night, becoming dirty and tired. The cool April air helped them avoid excessive sweating. The earth moved easily and smelled dusky and rich with leaf mold.

They dug a hole four feet deep, then went inside to retrieve Edward's body. It was easier to tug and pull him when they did not have to see his face, so the women covered his head with the make-shift shroud and sewed it shut. Together the women were able to lift Edward, Elaisse taking his shoulders and Fern taking his feet. They carried the dead boy to the kitchen garden, and lowered him into the hole as gently as they could.

"Should we mark it with stones?" Fern asked, and Elaisse was reminded how Thomas Taylor had deferred to her back in London. She wondered why others seemed to feel she was a leader and someone with all the answers.

"No, we can't mark it as a grave," Elaisse said, "because then others will know he is here and that we didn't burn him. Others must not know he is here. Only we will know, and God, of course."

Fern thought a moment, then agreed. She saw the logic.

They lit a candle so they could read from the Bible. They took turns, reading prayers quietly and solemnly.

This is the second person I've buried, Elaisse thought. *I hope there will be no more.*

When they were done, they went back inside the cottage. It was getting cold, so Elaisse closed the two windows while Fern lit a cook fire.

"What are you going to do now?" Elaisse asked.

"I don't know," Fern said. "I haven't had time to look ahead. Providing there is an 'ahead' at all for anyone."

"Come back to the castle with me," Elaisse offered. "My father is not there, so you'll be a guest, not a servant. There's nothing for you in the village anymore. Please, I need a friend, and so do you. Come back to Wynham Castle with me first thing in the morning."

Fern was quiet for a moment, then asked, "What about your brother Henry?"

"The law is specific that when the lord dies, the wife assumes the role as the lady of the castle. In England, a woman can even be a queen, and Matilda almost became one. Anyway, if my mother were to die, then Henry would rule. But my mother is still alive. And even if she weren't, and Henry did rule, I would still inherit the right to live in the castle with a salary. It is my birthright."

When Fern did not respond, Elaisse continued, "I have a say in matters of consequence. And I say for you to come and live at Wynham Castle. Will you?"

Fern smiled a wan smile. "Of course you are right. I have no family left, so I can't stay in this cottage. I'd be alone here and I don't want to be alone with the ghosts of this house. And I can't use the kitchen garden anymore—so thank you, yes."

And so plans were made.

In the morning, they walked together on the road leading back to the castle. Before they reached the end of the village, they noticed three children holding hands and pacing in a circle.

The children were singing a song:

Ring around the rosie,
Pockets full of posies,
Ashes, ashes,
We all fall down!

The two women exchanged glances. They understood the meaning of what would first appear as a nonsensical nursery rhyme.

The pockets full of posies signified the attempts to sweeten the air, as the villagers carried fragrant dried flowers and herbs in their pockets. The ashes represented Henry's decree that the bodies be burned. And 'we all fall down' characterized death.

Even if these children survived the Great Dying, they would be emotionally scarred forever.

Chapter Twelve

"Bring out your dead!"

The man walked beside the horse-drawn wagon through the deeply rutted lane that ran through the center of the village. He called out repeatedly to the cottages as he passed them.

The streets had been untended for so long that they had deteriorated. He felt the cart heave and then realized it had stopped abruptly.

He put his shoulder to the back of the cart while the horse pulled in front, and he urged the horse forward because the wagon was stalled in a pothole. A spring rain started, but the man was not worried about his cargo. The bodies piled in his wagon were oblivious to any weather conditions.

As the wagon lurched out of the pothole, the man reflected that Henry Sheffield was paying him to push the wagon through the village next to Wynham Castle. He felt the job was easier than plowing the fields. He knew that some of the fields were left to go fallow this spring because there weren't enough people to tend them, and what farmers remained had to take on a disproportionate amount of the labor required to plant any crop at all.

"Bring out your dead!"

The man continued his eerie calling, and was rewarded when two villagers brought a lifeless body to the wagon and threw the dead person on board. The man with the wagon purposely turned his head so he didn't have to watch as the new body tumbled on top of the others.

Once the body was secure enough not to fall off the wagon, the villagers disappeared like smoke and the man with the wagon continued his journey. Today the wagon only contained half a load. The man didn't know if that was because the disease was slowing or if there simply weren't enough people left in the village to fill the wagon.

Turning the horse around, the man pushed his cargo of death to the edge of the village. Once there, he positioned the wagon at a steep angle to dump his load, and looked elsewhere as stiff and unyielding bodies tumbled off the pushcart down to the scorched patch of earth below.

The man figured the light spring rain would soon stop. When it did, he would start another bonfire.

Early May 1349

Elaisse settled Fern in her old room. Then she went to see Henry. She found her brother once again in the dining hall, a glass of wine in his hand.

"That wine bottle seems permanently attached to your arm," she commented. "Does it travel with you everywhere?"

"I have court jesters to make me laugh, so I don't need you for the job," Henry said.

She sat at the long, heavy oak table which was covered with a linen tablecloth as usual. She noted that the cloth, usually immaculate, was now dotted with spills. Distracted for a moment by the appearance of the cloth, Elaisse wondered how it could be cleaned. She had once seen a maid wash the table linen. The maid had soaked it in a large wooden trough similar to the ones from which the horses drank, then rubbed it furiously with soap and vinegar before rinsing it and soaking it again. Elaisse realized she had never really considered the amount of work it entailed to do everyday maintenance for the castle.

She looked around, noticing layers of dust collecting upon just about everything. She saw that the straw and rushes upon the floor hadn't been changed in what appeared to be a very long time. The fireplace was not lit, but layer upon layer of wood coals and ashes were piled into what was becoming a very tall accumulation indeed. Some of the candles on the walls were burned to the quick, and no one had replaced them. She knew without having to look that no one would be in the kitchen and that it would be a mess.

"We'll have to cook our own meals," she observed.

"I'm drinking mine," Henry said.

"Listen, we have to talk."

"Dear Sister, I talk and *you* listen. That's the new rule around here."

Elaisse tried again. She came to the point. "Easter has come and gone, and Hocktide is over. You know that Hocktide should have been the beginning of the planting season. We need to start getting organized. We should take public polls to see who is well, and who can prepare the fields for the crops."

"The servants have all run away. The ones that didn't die, that it. As it stands, I'm paying an exorbitant amount of money to the guard to entice him to stay. So, dearest Sister, what do you suggest? How would we go about taking your public poll?" Henry drained his glass and poured another.

Elaisse felt encouraged because at least her brother appeared to be listening. She ignored his sarcasm and continued, "Yesterday I went into the village. A lot of the peasants are sick. The doctors are either gone or dead."

"Is that supposed to be news to me?" Henry put down his glass and appeared greatly annoyed. "I'm doing what I can for the villagers. I'm paying an enormous amount to the wagon-man to make sure he continues to carry out the dead."

She paused to take a breath and calm herself. Then she continued, "I believe that there are a lot of sick people who cannot respond to the wagon-man's calls. He doesn't look inside the cottages to see who has died."

"So?"

"So the wagon-man just passes by the cottages where dead people lay inside. The weather is getting warmer, and warm weather does bad things to dead bodies."

"And just who is going to peek inside these cottages? You?"

Has he always been this difficult? Elaisse wondered. Then she realized that she really didn't know her brother very well. He had, after all, been sent away to school and to military employment since he was seven, only coming home for visits on holidays over the years.

Elaisse continued, "I was thinking that we could go into the village and recruit a law enforcement crew. We could make them freemen and pay them with silver. We could offer them parcels of land as endowments."

"How you freely spend the castle's money," Henry said, "which as you know, is now my money."

She tried to control her rising frustration. "Henry, these are desperate times. We need to be creative in our efforts to restore some sort of normalcy. We need to recruit villages and we need to be able to depend upon their loyalty. This will come at a price. We need to be willing to pay that price. If we don't get the dead out of the cottages before the weather warms even more, the price will be higher than money—the price will be more death. If we allow the dead to bake in the heat...well, let's just say I don't want to imagine the results of that."

"I have already thought of that, so I don't need a mere woman's input," Henry said, and she knew he was lying. He had not even considered it. But as long as the deeds got done, Elaisse was not interested in who got the credit for thinking of it first.

So she pretended he had not spoken and continued, "Perhaps, out of compassion, we should hold Bible services for the dead. Actually, the services would be more to comfort the living. That way, the villagers could pray for their dead. We could appoint someone to attend who would be a representative from the castle. All in all, these services would be another step in becoming organized. We need to build up the morale of the peasants so they can look to the future. As it is now, they are immobile with grief and I can't say as I blame them."

"Well, you're such a woman of action," Henry sneered.

Continuing to ignore his comments, she asked, "So you will get started with these things right away?"

"Of course. Now go away and let me drink my wine in peace."

She rose from the table and left the room. She went to find Fern, to see if her friend was getting settled back at Wynham without difficulty. When she found her, she invited Fern to take a walk on the castle grounds.

Outside, the new growth of grass was a lime-green in color, and the trees were sprouting their young leaves. The early crabapples were already flush with pink flowers, and the wind carried the petals to decorate the grounds like spilled confetti. The birds sang with a joyous melody, seeming to be happy that the earthworms were coming back to the surface of the earth as the soil warmed. The fragrant wild violets nodded their heads in the soft spring breeze.

"It's so beautiful here," Elaisse commented to Fern as the two women meandered through the castle grounds.

"Remember that you once told me that you'd be back when the leaves grew once again?" Fern asked.

Elaisse reminisced. "Yes, that was when I was planning to run away to London. How long ago that seems! Back then, I couldn't possibly have foreseen all that was about to happen in the world. I've decided that you just cannot plan life, because life goes its own way and creates its own plans. It doesn't ask us what we would prefer it to do."

"Sir Geoffrey Gladden is dead," Fern said.

Elaisse stopped walking. "From the pestilence?"

"He is probably the only one who has died from something else. He got drunk and took a fall. At least, that is what everyone is saying. Speaking of getting drunk, I should tell you that the gossip is spreading about your brother's drinking habits."

Elaisse was incredulous. "With all this death and disease around us, people still find time to gossip?"

Fern smiled ruefully. "It's human nature to gossip. The villagers are resentful that they are getting no assistance. They feel ignored by the castle during their time of need. That's why they talk amongst themselves about Henry Sheffield."

They began walking again, and headed towards the wall that separated the castle grounds from the forest. Suddenly Fern cried, "Look!"

"What?"

"Over there!" Fern pointed. "Look, there's someone sitting on the castle wall!"

Elaisse realized there was indeed a man sitting on top of the wall, his legs dangling over on the side facing the castle. Without the usual guards patrolling, it was obviously not impossible to climb up the seven feet of stone. The man seemed quite content to stay where he was, because he made no move to come down.

She squinted, trying to see better. The man had blonde hair that shone in the sunlight, similar to her own. He appeared tall, young and rugged. Something about his mannerisms and movements struck a familiar chord deep within Elaisse's very being. She gasped with recognition, even though she was still quite a distance away from the man on the wall.

She stopped walking as a sensation of heat flushed her face. She felt her heart drop like a stone and she wanted to fall to her knees to collect herself. She remained standing but her legs threatened to collapse, and she trembled with dizziness. Her mouth was dry as her scratchy woolen cloak and in contrast her eyes were wet.

Fern noticed and became alarmed. "What's the matter? Do you know that man?"

"Yes, I know him. Go back to the castle and I will see you there later." With that, Elaisse began running towards the man she loved.

Seeing her coming, Roger waved but made no effort to come down off the wall. When she got close, she could see he was grinning. Always grinning, and always laughing at inappropriate times. That was Roger, and how glad she was to see him!

She reached the base of the wall. She told him to come down.

"No, *you* come up here," Roger laughed.

"Oh, you are so contrary!" she scolded, and it was as if they had never separated.

She stood at the bottom of the wall and waited, but still Roger made no effort to climb down. He continued to sit and grin, dangling his legs over the side of the wall, kicking his heels against the stones.

"Aren't you coming down?" Elaisse asked, exasperated.

"I told you, you're coming up." Roger moved to lie on top of the wall, his arms outstretched to reach for her. "Here, grab my hands. I'll help you climb."

It was a dare and she knew it. He had often told her that he admired her spirit, and now he was testing how much spirit she had. She stretched for his hands and could barely reach his fingers.

Then she thought, *To hell with being proper*. She started to climb up the rock wall, surprised at how easy it was to find handholds and footholds.

He grabbed her arms and lifted her. She was pulled to the top of the castle wall, and was suddenly seated beside him. They sat side-by-side, both quietly relishing the fact that they were together again. They didn't speak but simply savored the nearness of the other.

None of this seemed real, and she feared she would wake from a dream. Her heart quickened when Roger put his arm around her shoulders, drawing her to him. Together they sat, still silent, looking at the castle grounds and enjoying the moment.

Finally Elaisse spoke. "How did you know Fern and I would be out walking today?"

"I didn't know," he said. "But this isn't the first time I've sat on this wall."

"What do you mean?"

"I've sat here many times over the past week, hoping to see you." He held her closer. "I've been waiting for you. I knew I'd see you sooner or later. And you were certainly worth the wait."

She smiled, feeling incredibly happy. Every time she was with Roger, the stress and fear of the Great Dying seemed to diminish; to melt away from her heart.

And then he started to rise. "Listen, Beautiful...let's take a walk through the forest."

"The forest?" she asked, but found herself standing up along with him on top of the wall.

"Well, I'm certainly not going to parade around inside the castle grounds and tell everybody that I want to kidnap the princess."

"I'm not a princess," Elaisse said primly, "and you cannot kidnap someone who goes willingly. But how will we get down?"

"Climbing down is easier than climbing up."

He helped her down, and when they reached the ground they held hands as they entered the woods. This time of year the undergrowth was sparse because the bushes had not completely filled out with their summer splendor. Sunlight filtered easily through the trees, and decaying leaves from the previous season littered the trail and created a musty scent that filled their nostrils. The day was warm with a periodic cool breeze, rustling the branches of the shrubbery that was flush with spring sap.

They walked a ways, then Roger led her to a green meadow that was fairly dry because it basked in the spring sunshine. She saw his horse was here, tied to a tree; it was the same bay gelding he had ridden for as long as she had known him. He went to his horse and retrieved a woolen blanket from the saddlebag and spread it on the grass in the center of the sunlit meadow. Neither spoke; it was as if they didn't want the magic spell of the place to be broken. Everything seemed to have a dreamlike quality.

She understood his intentions and made no move to stop him. Her desires were as great as his, and she longed for his touch. He laid her back on the blanket and made love to her. They had a part of the blanket covering their nakedness, and neither noticed when it slipped off.

Afterwards they lay together on top of the blanket, the forest floor soft and yielding. "I've missed you," he told her.

Elaisse held him tighter and Roger cradled her in his arms. He pulled the blanket back over them.

"I'm never leaving you again," he said.

She rose up on one elbow. "How can I believe you?"

He didn't answer so she reached for her clothes; although a warm day for the time of year, it was still too cold to be naked. She refused to meet his eyes as she got up and dressed. He began to put his clothes on as well.

Once dressed, he pulled her back down on the blanket until they were sitting face-to-face. "You were all I could think about, night and day," he told her. "I had to come back to see if you'd give me another chance. No other woman has ever held me spellbound like you do. Elaisse, could you ever find it in your heart to love me again?"

"You've left me twice."

"That's because I was twice a fool," he said. "I didn't want to admit to myself that you've changed my life. I thought I could just continue as before. But there's nothing in this world as it was before. Nothing!"

"I know that," she said. "I've tried to tell you that myself."

He continued, "The Great Dying has taught me a new perspective; a new set of values. It changes a man to realize he is in love. So I ask you again, can you find it in your heart to love me once more?"

Elaisse looked directly into his eyes, her gaze unfaltering as she searched for answers. "I love you. I've never stopped loving you. I've loved you for what seems like a long time now. Surely you know that. But how can I trust you?"

He took a deep breath, then said, "I've never told you before that I would never leave you. But I'm telling you that now. I've never told you before that I love you. But I'm telling you that now, too. I'm asking for your hand in marriage."

She was stunned. Then she realized something and told him, "There are no priests. So you can safely ask me all you want, knowing there is no way we could really marry."

He threw back his head and laughed. She was so mad that she hit him in the arm.

"Oh Elaisse," he laughed, ignoring her punch, "no one can ever get anything past you, can they? But I know where there *is* a priest. If you agree to marry me, I will take you to him."

"Okay then, where is this priest?"

"Hiding. I stumbled across him the other day. You'd be surprised at how many people are hiding all over England's countryside, camping in the forests or dwelling in caves. I know where this priest is hiding, and I can flush him out for us. In fact, I believe he is a bishop who ran away from his flock in London."

"Imagine being married by a coward," she said, then to call his bluff, she added, "Maybe I could prepare for a wedding within a week."

Laughing, Roger bent down, picked Elaisse up, and lifted her onto his shoulder. Carrying her, he walked to his horse and then placed her onto the gelding's rump. The horse shied a bit, then settled down. Roger went back to roll up the blanket, and with Elaisse holding on tightly behind him, flicked the reins so that the horse started forward.

"Where are you taking me?" Elaisse asked.

"Why wait until next week? I'm taking you to the priest now."

She hit him again, this time in the shoulder. "Oh Roger, are you never serious?"

"I'm very serious," he said.

"I'm not going to marry you today! Please take me back to the castle; take me to the front gate this time."

He reined his horse, changing direction. When they arrived at the castle gate, he dismounted and helped her down.

"When can I see you again?" he asked.

"Come to the light meal at six o'clock. We only have one guard left, but I will instruct him to let you in. If you're serious about marrying me, then you will have to meet my mother and my brother. But for goodness sakes, please behave when you do!"

"I'll just be myself," he told her. "That way, your family will be sure to love me."

She rolled her eyes as he rode off.

Chapter Thirteen

Deaths from the bubonic plague played havoc with the economy of England. The immense depopulation made for fewer workers, who in turn demanded and received higher wages. Any landowner that refused to make concessions was often unpleasantly surprised when the labor force vanished to castles that contained more generous landlords.

Panicked, Parliament met in 1349 to pass an ordinance as an attempt to prevent peasants from transplanting their services and their loyalties. But this proved hard to enforce, and landowners found themselves forced to lease out the land without receiving a share of the crops and without any promised services. The peasants found a new individuality in this practice as they could farm the leased land and keep the proceeds of their labor themselves, although they still had to pay rent.

But while almost everyone knew how to farm, other jobs required special skills and there were simply not enough knowledgeable citizens left to do the work at any price. These jobs included ironworkers, priests, artists, ship builders, and certain manufacturers.

Salt was essential during the Middle Ages as a preserving agent for many foods, and without salt miners, the population was left without the means to store meat. Other essential specialty professions were not staffed either, so many goods disappeared.

Prices fluctuated wildly. Horses, cows and oxen lost value and could be bought very cheaply. Prices of grain also fell steeply, increasing the landowners' financial worries. On the other hand, the price of salt more than tripled. Embroidered and other fancy clothing became unobtainable, and anything that needed to be transported or manufactured became extremely expensive.

The bubonic plague created a situation that was, in essence, the end of the bartering system in England. The use of money instead of trade came to the forefront as feudalism went by the wayside.

Mid-May 1349

A breathless and excited Fern greeted Elaisse inside the castle door. "I have such news!" she exclaimed.

Elaisse had never seen Fern this ecstatic. "What?"

"It's John Wythe!" Fern cried. "John Wythe is here at the castle!"

Stunned, Elaisse froze. Sounds seemed muffled because of the loud ringing in her ears. She felt a thumping in her chest, but was so lightheaded that she was afraid for a moment that she would faint. Her fingers tingled and her forehead felt clammy.

"John is alive? That's impossible. My father told me he was killed in France."

"Your father wanted you to marry Sir Geoffrey," Fern said. "He probably wanted you to stop thinking about John Wythe. Maybe your father felt that by the time you found out that John was still alive, you'd already be married to Geoffrey Gladden."

"I can't believe my father lied to me."

"Are you all right?" Fern asked. "I feel confused at your reaction."

"I...I just can't believe it."

"But aren't you glad he's here?"

"Well...I'm glad he's alive."

"What?"

How could Elaisse admit she was now in love with someone else? "It's been a long time, and a lot has happened since I've last spoken to him."

"Aren't you going to see him?"

"Yes, of course I'll see him. Where is he?"

"In the large dining hall with your brother."

Elaisse thanked Fern, then went down the corridor to the main room. She paused outside the entrance for a moment to collect her wits. Then, taking a deep breath, she entered.

There he was, seated across the table from her brother. John, the man she at one time was sure she loved, was alive. He was talking to Henry, but as soon as she entered the room, all conversation stopped.

John looked a little older, and a little thinner. But otherwise he looked the same, with his wavy brown hair and dark eyes that crinkled at the corners when he smiled. He looked at her in amazement and told her, "Elaisse, you are more beautiful than ever."

She ran to him and he stood up. He took her in his arms and hugged her as tightly as he could without hurting her.

"I thought you were dead!" she told him, blinking back tears.

"Didn't I tell you I'd come home?" he asked. He held her for what seemed to be a long time. Then he pulled up a heavy oak chair for her and they both sat at the table, and she asked how he managed to leave France.

"The war is at a standstill because there is not enough military force on either side to continue," John explained. "King Edward III has called the troops back. In France, the people are in an uproar for Philip IV to stop the Great Dying. Obviously, he can't. So now France is unable to discipline its own troops, who are clamoring for Philip's son to take over the crown. The people in France, at least the ones still alive, seem demented, I swear to you. But now that I've come back to England, I see it isn't much better here. How lucky I am that God chose to spare you from the pestilence!"

"We're both lucky," Elaisse said. "I'm so glad you're safe."

"Now we can continue where we left off," John said. "Your father isn't here to stop us from marrying."

"My father told me you were killed in France."

Henry joined in, laughing loudly. "Our father obviously

didn't tell you the truth. Just one of many untruths, I'm sure."

"But why would he lie?" Elaisse asked.

"Because he didn't want us to marry," John said, looking at her closely. "He didn't think I was noble enough. But now that your father has gone to his Creator, you and I can go ahead with plans for marriage. Once you and I are legally wed, my status will become equal to yours."

"I don't think status matters anymore," Elaisse said.

"Of course it matters. Class always shows." Again he looked closely at her, studying her.

"Well, this is all so sudden."

"What is sudden? We've been waiting months to be together again."

Elaisse glanced nervously away, wondering what to do. Then she said, wanting to get away from Henry, "The weather is beautiful outside. Can we go for a walk?"

She took his hand and led him outside to the castle grounds. They strolled for a while without speaking, then he tried to kiss her, but Elaisse broke the embrace. Out of the corner of her eye, she scanned the castle walls, hoping desperately that no one would be seated there. She was grateful when no trace of Roger could be seen. She wondered, *How am I supposed to choose?*

John took both of her shoulders in his hands and forced her to face him. "What's going on here? What's the matter with you?"

"I thought you were dead," Elaisse stammered, not knowing what else to say.

"You've already said that," John reminded her. "Do you wish I were?"

"No! Of course not. It's just…"

John became impatient and angry. "Say what you mean! Right now!"

"Let me explain," she soothed, but inside she wondered, *How can I decide right now about something that will not only affect the rest of my life, but two other lives as well?*

She took his hand and they resumed their walk, stepping through the spring clover and the fragrant early violets that peeked between blades of new grass. "When you left, my father told me you were killed in France. He wanted me to marry Sir Geoffrey Gladden."

"So? I know all of that."

"Let me finish. I ran away to London because I refused to marry anyone but you. But then the pestilence struck, the Great Dying began, and the whole world changed."

"I told you I know all of that!" John yelled. "Get to the point!"

"Calm down and let me finish!" Elaisse took a deep breath. "I met someone. Someone who helped me."

John gripped her hand too tightly, hurting her. "Let me guess—that someone is another man. Who is he?"

"Let go of me—you're hurting me!"

John released her hand, then demanded again, "Who is he?"

"His name is Roger. That's all I know."

John stopped walking and stared at her. "What! What about his station in life? Is he at least an earl or a duke? What's his last name?"

"He never told me any of that." She blushed as she realized just how strange it sounded.

He gaped at her in disbelief. "He's a stranger to you?"

"It wasn't like that."

"Don't tell me he's a commoner!"

"I don't know for sure, but I think so. Anyway, what does status matter anymore?"

"I keep telling you that status will always matter!" He stomped away for a few steps, then turned around and walked back to face her. He seemed to be desperately trying to control himself.

Then he spoke more calmly and said in a quiet but firm voice, "Listen, Elaisse. It is understandable that the pestilence and the Great Dying have affected your judgment. All of us have been under great strain and a lot of us have temporarily lost our sense of reason."

"But—"

He cut her off. "I've been talking to Henry and he has agreed that once you and I wed, we will receive your share of the inheritance and I will help him get the peasants back in line. Henry and I will work to restore the tax system and bring the laborers back to the responsibilities that they owe to the castle. The fields need to be planted right now, so we need to get tough with the villagers."

"You are not going to find any cooperation from the villagers," Elaisse said. "And what of my mother? Have you forgotten that since my father's death, it is the Lady Hildred who now rules the castle?"

"Henry says your mother has gone daft. He's going to take care of her."

"I don't like the sound of that. 'Take care of her' could have two meanings, and I don't see Henry as very nurturing."

"Henry knows what he is doing!"

"Stop shouting at me."

John sighed. "Elaisse, forget this Roger fellow. I will forgive you for your indiscretions only since I can imagine what a strain you've been through. Now stop being silly, because we have a wedding to plan."

She turned to him as he walked beside her. "John, I can't marry you now. I need time to think—and to sort everything out."

He hissed at her, "And to think that I carried a lock of your hair with me in France."

He reached into his vest pocket, yanked out the hair, and threw it on the ground. He stepped on it, grinding it into the dirt. "Did you sleep with this Roger? Did he make you a harlot?"

Elaisse felt hot anger. "I don't have to answer that. And I am by no means a harlot, no matter what you think or say."

He reached for her, but she rejected his advances.

John sighed again. "Still pushing me away, I see. Just like that night in the barn. Well, for your information, I've had other women too. You're not the only one who wanted sex during the Great Dying. And there were a lot of women in France, many of whom were a lot happier to see me than you are. And they were just as pretty as you, if not prettier."

She felt stung, despite herself, but she didn't know if it was jealousy or the idea that he was purposely trying to hurt her.

He softened. "Listen," he told her, "maybe I do love you, or maybe I don't. Who can think straight these days? Let's face it, both of us have changed. We're not the innocents we were before the Great Dying. We've become hardened because of all the terrible things we've seen. But Elaisse, think about what makes sense here, right now."

"What?"

"We're alike, you and I. We are both of noble blood, and we are destined to be lord and lady over the villagers. Together we can make that happen. And I promise I'll be good to you. So no matter what you've done in my absence, I will forgive you because there are more important things to consider. Let's get married right away."

Elaisse thought frantically, *Is he right or wrong? How can I decide?*

She tried to call back the feelings that she thought she had once felt for John Wythe, but she could only remember that part of her life as though it were her childhood. After all that had happened since, it seemed like a lifetime ago.

Did she love John? Had she ever really loved John? Where at one point in her life she thought she could not live without him, now it felt as though he was a stranger. And when she thought he had died, he had truly died in her heart. If she were to reject him now, she would not mourn the loss of him, because she had already mourned him once before and let go of him back then. Her heart had begun anew with another man.

Suddenly it all became very clear.

Suddenly she knew how to choose.

With John, she had been infatuated. The only times she had spent with him were the few secret meetings in the stable.

But with Roger, she had lived daily for two months, learning his everyday habits. She knew Roger's good points and his bad, and felt him easy to get along with during both. She knew that Roger was someone who possessed good values about the meaning of life, and was someone who was strong in times of trouble and kind in times of well being.

But what had she ever learned about John? What did she really know about him?

She knew more about a man whose last name was unknown to her than this man walking beside her. What had she ever felt for John other than a physical attraction?

She told him, "John, I can't marry you."

He grabbed her shoulders and shook her violently, causing her hair to fly and her neck to snap forward and back. "You'd better think again!" he shouted.

"Stop it!" she cried.

He let her go, but his face was almost scarlet with rage. "You've lost your mind! The pestilence has driven you mad! You'd better reconsider, because you and Henry cannot run this castle without me. When you marry me, I will have legal rights over the peasants. Wake up and come to reality!"

He glared at her for a moment, and then stomped away. She watched him go before walking to the spot where the abandoned lock of hair lay. She stood for a moment, sadly looking at the golden hair that had been ground into the dirt.

Her head told her that everything John said made sense. The winds of change had blown, and order needed to be restored before the peasants either ran away or simply refused to work at all.

Marrying John would solve the business side of things; by giving John a title, they had a chance to pick up the pieces and preserve the old way of life—the only life she had ever known before the Great Dying.

But her heart told her that she longed for Roger's continued presence in her life.

Her heart also told her that feudalism held great disadvantages for people she cared about such as Fern and others like her. She felt the old ways could never be again.

160

This was a revolution where you couldn't put the pieces back together, because the pieces no longer fit in the puzzle of life. Perhaps the Great Dying would create better understandings between peasants and nobility.

She figured that there could be new solutions that no one had thought up yet, ones that might allow the peasants to own some parts of the land upon which they worked. Maybe the villagers could be given incentives to work and not just punishments if they didn't. There had to be a way where peasants could share the profits. There had to be a way where both sides could benefit from new rules in life.

And then her thoughts came back to the present, and she wondered what time it was. After all, Roger was supposed to arrive at six. She went inside the castle and learned it was now five o'clock.

She went into the dining hall and was surprised to see her mother there. Her brother was nowhere to be found, and Elaisse felt relieved, because when Henry and Hildred were in the same room together, they quarreled violently about control of the castle.

It was good to see Hildred up and about, because she had been experiencing headaches and nausea and was confined herself to her room. At first afraid that her mother had the pestilence, Elaisse relaxed when no buboes appeared. Hildred's sickness, although mysterious, was obviously not the same one that caused the Great Dying.

"How are you today?" Elaisse asked her mother.

"I don't think I'm quite well yet," Hildred said, and Elaisse noticed how drawn and haggard she appeared. "I came away from my room because I heard John Wythe is back and I wanted to welcome him. But now that I'm here, I don't think I'm up to it. I need to go back to bed because I feel so poorly."

Hildred tried to rise, and steadied herself with a hand on the back of a chair.

"Here, let me help you," Elaisse offered, very concerned. She took her mother's arm and helped her walk. When they reached

161

the room, Elaisse saw that the bed was unmade, the room in disarray, and a mug of cow's milk was on a saucer on the bedside table.

"Are you going to drink that?" Elaisse asked.

"No, it's been sitting here all day. Since I've been sick the past few days, Henry has been bringing my meals. Today I couldn't eat so he brought me that milk. Take it away, please."

Elaisse grabbed the mug, kissed her mother on the cheek, and left the room. She decided that she would go out to meet Roger herself instead of sending the guard. She took the mug of milk to the kitchen on her way outside.

Out in the castle grounds, she proceeded to the gate to meet Roger. She was surprised to see no guard there, and realized how difficult it really was to control the working class.

She opened the gate herself and went outside the castle grounds, leaving the gate ajar. The sun was setting and twilight was approaching rapidly but there was still enough light to see. She saw Roger before she heard him, and soon he was close enough for his horse's hooves to sound like thunder upon the ground. Roger approached at a fast clip and before she could collect her wits, he was right in front of her.

"What a wonderful welcome this is!" Roger laughed. "You've decided to guard the castle yourself? That would work because no one would want to go inside—they would simply stay out here to stare at you!"

She smiled despite herself. "Oh be serious. There's been a change in plans. I can't have dinner with you tonight. Can we make it tomorrow instead?"

"Probably for the best," he said.

"Why?"

"Because I'm not ready to meet your family yet. I told you before that I'm a scoundrel. I've done things in the past that might come back to haunt me. So I've decided to tell you everything *before* we marry, not afterwards. I don't want your family to recognize me before I have a chance to tell you all about it."

She looked at him, totally confused.

"Don't worry," Roger laughed. "I'm not going to grow horns and cloven hooves right before your eyes. Just know that I'm no different now than I was in Grayton. I just want to talk to you tomorrow, when we have more time."

"Well, I guess so," she said doubtfully. "I'll meet you tomorrow at noon, at this gate. Then you can explain why you'd be worried that I would think you could grow cloven hooves."

She went back inside the castle ground, leaving Roger to ride off alone.

Passing the kitchen, she noticed something on the floor. Thinking it was a rag, she entered to take a closer look.

It was not a rag on the floor. It was a kitten. And it was dead.

Gasping, Elaisse looked to see where she had left the mug of milk. She looked at it and saw it was empty.

The kitten had drunk the milk. And it had died.

Suddenly Elaisse knew the truth. Henry had been giving poisoned milk to their mother.

She thought, *I have to check on my mother.*

Chapter Fourteen

As the populations thinned in England, the attitudes of the surviving peasants changed. They were no longer willing to accept a subservient role in the larger scheme of life. Whispers of discontent began circulating among the peasants in response to an increasing financial tax burden placed upon them. The lower classes grumbled amongst themselves, and they discussed how they could bring their grievances to the attention of the nobility.

The administrative incompetence of the government in their handling of the disposal of the dead added to the tensions. In increasing numbers, the lower classes began making demands upon the nobility: the end of serfdom, the right to fair wages, and the right to rent land at fair rates. The peasants argued that since everyone was a descendent from Adam and Eve, there should be an equality of all men under the King.

Massive tax evasions were becoming commonplace. The nobility countered this movement by increasing the investigations and the resulting punishments of offending peasants. This in turn only led to more peasants banding together in organized protests against the government. One English minister, John Ball, was imprisoned three times for repeatedly urging his parishioners towards mutiny in his anti-government sermons.

Groups of clandestine rebels organized to lead the underclass in defiance of the oppression of serfdom.

One of these rebel leaders was Roger Browne, the man that Elaisse knew simply as Roger.

Late May 1349

Elaisse raced out of the kitchen into the hallway, but her foot caught in her skirt and she tumbled to the floor. Dazed for a moment, she was sickened by the straw and rushes on the floor that had been left so long without replacement that they had become foul. She got to her feet and held herself to a walk because the drafty hallway was dark due to the numerous candles that had burned to the quick and were no longer lit.

She went to her mother's bedroom and stood for a moment outside the door. She was afraid of what she might find within, because she imagined the lifeless body of her mother instead of the kitten. But she had to know: *Did Henry poison our mother?*

With that thought, she took a deep breath and entered the bedroom. Her first impression was again that the room was in disarray; clothes lay rumpled on a chair, a curtain from the canopy was hung incorrectly, and some of the bed linen had fallen onto the floor. And on table was another mug, this time empty of milk.

Her hands went to her mouth as she stifled a frightened gasp. She forced herself to look at her mother lying on the bed. Hildred was on her back, very still, mostly covered with a blanket. What Elaisse seemed to focus upon was the bare chalk-white arm of her mother, which was outstretched, uncovered, and it dangled over the side of the bed, fingers seemingly pointing...accusing.

Elaisse shook herself into action. She ran to her mother and felt her forehead. It was still warm, but Elaisse could see no movements of her mother's chest rising to take any breaths. She felt her mother's neck and could find no pulse. Desperate, Elaisse grabbed her mother's hand mirror and held it under Hildred's nose.

The mirror did not fog.

Her mother took no breaths.

Her mother was dead.

With a cry, Elaisse dropped the hand mirror on the dirty floor and it shattered into hundreds of shards. It seemed to fall in slow motion as pieces of crystal glass tumbled to create winking points of light upon the floor. The bedroom was brightly lit with multitudes of candles, causing Hildred's arm to almost shine with grotesque whiteness as though the underbelly of a fish.

Unable to bear to look at the single accusing arm, Elaisse took it and moved it, placing it under the blanket. The stiffness of death had not yet set, so the arm moved easily. Hildred must have died within the last hour.

Now is not the time to mourn, Elaisse thought. *Now is the time to seek justice and to find my brother for whom my mother's lifeless arm points.*

She raced out of her mother's bedroom into the cold, dark passageway. She tripped again on her dress which had torn from her earlier fall. Angrily she ripped the material away from her feet, severing the torn part of her dress and dropping it on the floor. She did not want anything to get in the way of her mission: to stand before her brother and accuse him or murder.

Elaisse made her way down the main castle stairwell, dark and damp. She could hear sounds of dripping water that seeped from within the cracks of the masonry. She could smell the assault of stale air heavy with the scent of chamber pots and candle soot. Her senses seemed heightened, and even in the dim light she could see the dull shine of the wet stone stairs.

She found Henry in the dining room where he seemed to spend most of his time as of late, the never-empty glass of wine attached to his hand. He looked up when she entered the room, and Elaisse could tell by his expression that he was very drunk.

"You're a murderer!" she hissed at him.

"And you're a fool," he answered.

"How could you kill our mother?"

"She was in the way of my title."

Elaisse was dumbfounded. "So you admit to murder?"

"She died of the pestilence." Henry's face was impassive. "Our mother was sick, and she was just another victim of the Great Dying. You cannot prove otherwise."

"Yes, I *can* prove otherwise. She has no buboes. And—I

know for a fact that you poisoned her milk. I'm going to the authorities with my proof. Murderers are hanged."

Henry laughed drunkenly. "Only murderers who are caught are hanged."

Elaisse turned around, prepared to walk out of the room. And that was the last thing she remembered, because Henry rose from his chair, came up behind her, and struck her in the head with his wine bottle.

««—»»

The first thing Elaisse was aware of was the intense bolt of pain that throbbed on the left side of her head. Waves of nausea came and went, and she was momentarily afraid she would be sick, but that passed as she regained consciousness by degrees.

The second thing was that she could not see. At first frightened, she calmed herself with the realization that there was nothing wrong with her eyes; instead, wherever she was had no light source whatsoever and was intensely dark.

Gradually, as her mind cleared of its confusion and dizziness, she realized that her feet were bound together and so were her hands. It felt like some sort of strong rope-like material was holding her feet and hands, tied tightly enough to prevent escape, but not tight enough to cut off circulation.

She was cold and she sat on stone, which told her that she must be on the lowest floor of the castle, the floor that usually housed the servants. It was the floor she had never explored because she had always considered it the basement: a dark, damp, and scary place indeed.

What happened? Why was she here?

She thought hard, and tried to recall the circumstances that led up to this terrible situation. How long had she been unconscious? She felt stiff as though she had been sitting in a single position for hours, so it must have been a while. Her mouth was dry and she had an incredible thirst.

Then she remembered—Henry! He had murdered their mother with poison.

She wondered, *How did I get down here, wherever I am?*

The only logical conclusion was that Henry must have somehow overpowered her and put her in the dark castle cellar. And she felt chilled as she realized that her brother was without conscience, and if he were cold and calculating enough to kill their mother, what would he do with her?

In fact, why wasn't she dead already? Why hadn't Henry simply murdered her as he had Hildred?

She tested the ropes which held her and realized that Henry made no mistakes when he tied them. Elaisse was bound fast and there would be no escape that way.

Unless—could she find a stone that was sharp enough to rub the ropes against? She was leaning against a stone wall, and wondered if her solution could be found there.

But then another wave of dizziness overwhelmed her, and she lost consciousness again. She was unaware that when Henry hit her on the head with the thick, heavy wine bottle, he had caused a concussion.

«—»

Later that night, John Wythe knew he would find Henry drinking in the dining hall, which was where Henry always seemed to be. John strode into the room and said, "We need to talk about Elaisse."

Henry pulled out a chair for his friend and said, "Sit down and have a drink."

John sat but he was adamant that they discuss Elaisse. "I don't want a drink. I want to talk about your sister. I asked for her hand in marriage and she refused me!"

Henry smiled. In frustration, John sputtered, "Didn't you hear what I said?"

"Don't worry," Henry said. "I keep telling you that I always have things under control, but you are so impatient. My mother died tonight of the pestilence. Her body is still in her room and we will need to summon the guard to remove and burn her remains. So, now I am lord of Wynham Castle!"

"Well," John said, "I don't know if condolences or congratulations are in order. But what about me? I am only an earl unless your sister agrees to marry me. And I have no land unless I join your bloodline."

"I think my sister is now in a position to reconsider."

"What do you mean? Have you spoken to her?"

"I did more than that. She seems to have this ridiculous idea that I am somehow responsible for our mother's death."

John studied Henry closely, then asked, "Are you?"

"I am going to need your loyalty if we are to keep this castle," Henry said, ignoring the question. "In return, you will be placed in a position of wealth and power. Isn't that what you want?"

John looked at the table, unable to meet Henry's eyes. "Yes."

"So whether I killed my mother or not is none of your concern, right?" Henry paused for a minute, then added, "If you really must know, my mother died of the pestilence. But you must never question me again, ever, about anything."

John looked up, relieved, believing Henry. "I won't question you again. That's a promise. Now, what did you say to Elaisse?"

"I didn't say anything to her. I have her tied up in the wine cellar."

"What!"

Henry took a drink with one hand and waved the other in the air in a gesture of dismissal. "She was agitated and hysterical. She was unreasonable. I lost my temper and popped her one over the head. Don't worry, I didn't hurt her. But she's being restrained until she comes to her senses."

John was aghast. "We've got to get her out!"

"Not so fast. First, I have a plan."

"What plan? Henry, this is kidnapping."

"You'd better listen to me," Henry said, "because I'm in charge here. Nobody knows where Elaisse is but you and me. She can either agree to marry you or she can stay where she is and rot there for all I care. It would be easy to explain her death as just another casualty of the Great Dying. Who would question it?"

"Henry," John said slowly. "You know this isn't right."

"If you think like that, you will ruin both of our lives, yours and mine. Listen up, John, because I need your help to manage the peasants. This is your only chance for a title and land. Don't waste this opportunity."

Suddenly John found himself not so much concerned with Elaisse's welfare as he was with his own future. "Do you think she'll see reason?" he asked hopefully.

"She has to if she ever wants to see the sunlight again."

"I promise I'll give her a good life. Henry, I have to make her see that I'd give her anything she wants—all I want in return is a title and land. Is that so unreasonable?"

"I'd say she'd be a damn lucky woman to be your wife."

««—»»

Elaisse came awake again. She had been alternating in and out of consciousness for a while, but gradually she was beginning to feel more stable. Her legs ached from her sitting position, and her back was cold and damp from leaning against the stone wall.

She wanted to get her bearings. She sniffed the air to see what it could tell her about her location. She could smell a rich fruity fragrance mixed with a scent of mold. It seemed familiar and Elaisse felt that she should know that smell but it was just out of her mental reach.

She tried to see in the darkness. There was no light of any kind; no sunlight streaming through any windows or peeking through any cracks in the walls. It was completely and totally dark—as dark as a tomb; as dark as death.

Perhaps she was in some place of storage?

Of course—that fruity, moldy smell. She was in the wine cellar!

It gave her some sense of comfort, because she knew that Henry was a frequent visitor to the wine cellar. Maybe she could reason with him when he came down to replenish his supply. In the meantime, she resumed her task of rubbing the rope against the rough stone wall, hoping against hope that she could fray the rope apart.

170

Suddenly she stopped to listen. She could swear she heard a sound, but when she strained her ears to listen again, there was nothing.

There! Elaisse heard the slight sound again. She could hear a faint rustling, and the fine hairs on her arms prickled as goosebumps caused them to rise. Was she alone in the dungeon that was the wine cellar?

Then she froze, because suddenly she knew. She was sure she knew what made the slight rustling sound.

Rats!

There were rats in the wine cellar.

Elaisse sucked in her breath. Visions of vermin in the streets of London haunted her. She pictured the rats coming at her in the darkness, getting closer, and crouching in their approach. Were the rats hungry? Hungry enough to bite a woman who was unable to defend herself because her hands and feet were bound?

Frantically Elaisse went back to rubbing her ropes against the stone wall. She had to get free. She could hear the rats coming closer, as if they were getting used to her presence and were becoming braver because of it.

My God in Heaven! she thought when she felt a tickling at her leg. It was too dark to see, but Elaisse's dress had been torn away from one of her legs and she could feel the rodent's whiskers as the rat sniffed her flesh.

A moan escaped her, and she lifted both legs together as a unit and swung as hard as she could against where she felt the rat. She heard a startled squeak, and took satisfaction that she must have hit her target.

She knew her margin of safety wouldn't last because the rats would recoup. They would approach her again, and soon. Elaisse methodically resumed rubbing her ropes against the stone wall. She had to get free. She tried to keep her ears finely tuned to any sounds that would indicate the rats would try to stalk her again.

Minutes passed as she continued to grind the rope against the wall. Was it her imagination or did the rope binding her hands feel loser?

She heard the rats approach again. This time it sounded like more than one. She could hear their little nails scrabbling on the stone floor. She could hear a faint rustling and an occasional squeak.

"Shoo!" Elaisse shouted, and the rats quieted, but only for a moment. They seemed to sense that she could not defend herself. The rats were getting bolder.

Again she felt the whiskers against her bare calf. She tried to kick, but a rat unexpectedly leapt on her leg. With a cry, Elaisse dropped to a prone position and rolled, trying to shake off the rat that clung to her calf.

Suddenly the rope binding her hands broke apart. Her hands were free!

She sat up and shoved the rat off her leg. She grabbed the rope and started swinging it towards the rats. Again she heard a startled squeal which told her that the rope had lashed out and connected.

With her hands free, Elaisse felt more in control. She used the rope as a weapon and kept swinging it to keep the rats at bay. She didn't know how she would be able to both fight the rats and remove the remaining rope around her ankles at the same time.

Then she heard a completely different sound. Someone was coming! She could hear the wine cellar door opening and could see a shape holding a candle.

"Henry!" she cried. "Get me out of here!"

Instead of her brother, a female voice spoke. "Elaisse! Keep your voice low."

It was Fern. Somehow, Fern had found her. "There are rats down here," Elaisse said.

Fern held up the candle and the rats fled from the light. "Did any of them bite you?"

"I don't think so," Elaisse said.

Fern came to her side and crouched. She tried to untie the rope at Elaisse's ankles, but they were bound tightly. "I heard Henry and John talking," Fern explained as she worked the rope. "I spied on them. That's how I knew you were here."

172

The ropes came free. "Let's get out of here," Elaisse said.

"There are new guards," Fern warned. "Henry has recruited four more."

"I've got to get a horse and ride to London," Elaisse said. "I can petition the authorities to review my mother's death. If they find Henry guilty, which he is, then he can be hanged."

"You would hang your own brother?"

"He murdered my mother."

"I understand," Fern said. "Henry is many evil things, and a murderer is just one of his evils, although it is the worst. But how will you get past the guards?"

"Don't you know them?"

"The new guards have been paid so well that I am not sure I can influence them."

"Let's go to the servants' quarters," Elaisse said. "I'll hide out there until I can think of a way to escape."

The two women sneaked up the cellar steps. When they reached the passageway that led out of the wine cellar, Elaisse realized it was dawn. She had been a prisoner in the dark basement all night.

Chapter Fifteen

The church leaders in London were threatening the priest John Ball with excommunication for his advocacy of "social equality." John of Gaunt, who was the brother of King Edward III, was an aggressive coordinator in the suppression of the underclass and he played a paramount role in the repeated imprisonment of Father Ball.

To further confuse the legal issues, most 14th Century English laws were either written in Latin or in "law language." Most of the educated persons who were able to read and understand the laws died in the plague epidemic. That meant that interpretations became convoluted and the nobility used that to their advantage against the peasants.

But the efforts of the nobility could not suppress the growing momentum of the peasants' unrest. The movement gained strength at the hands of an underprivileged man named Wat Tyler, whose efforts to organize the underclass of England was succeeding rapidly due to Tyler's charismatic manner and his effective speeches.

Roger Browne was Tyler's associate, and his role was to aid the flight of peasants from oppressive landlords and to lead them to Essex, where Tyler resided.

An underground system of escaping peasants was carefully structured and maintained. Meanwhile, Wat Tyler spread his dissident movement to Kent, with eventual plans to take London by storm. Plans were made for the seizure of the Tower of London, capturing the archbishop of Canterbury and other officials in the process. Tyler knew he could count on Roger Browne for help when the time came to make the plan work.

Early June 1349

At noon, Roger waited at the main gate outside the castle grounds. His horse was impatient and stamped its feet and shook its head frequently, jangling its bridle. Finally Roger dismounted, and tied his horse to the same shrub that he had waited behind so many months before when he helped Elaisse run away to London.

It had rained briefly the night before, but now the sun shined brightly with the promise of another lovely day. It was the first of June and Roger was anxious to spend this day with the woman he loved. He was finally ready to confess his secrets.

If he told her who and what he was, would she condemn his role in the peasant insurrection against the upper classes? Or would she understand?

Roger continued to worry as time passed and still Elaisse did not show. What was keeping her from their meeting? He began to feel afraid that perhaps she had changed her mind; perhaps she had decided she didn't want to spend her life with him after all. But Roger remembered the love that had showed in her eyes when they were together, and so he refused to believe that she could stop loving him now.

He waited another half hour, and still she did not come. He felt a rising apprehension. What had happened? What caused Elaisse to be so late in meeting him when she promised to be there?

And then Roger asked himself, *What should I do if she doesn't show up at all?*

Soon the position of the sun told him it was around two in the afternoon. He decided it was time to stop waiting and to start figuring things out. He walked to the same place where he had sat on the wall the previous day. He climbed the seven feet of stone and sat on top, scanning the castle grounds for any sign of

Elaisse.

He sat on the wall for about twenty minutes, and was frustrated when he saw no one. He had to decide what to do. *To hell with caution*, Roger thought. *I'm going to find out what happened to Elaisse. If she wants to get rid of me, she will have to tell me to my face.*

And so Roger climbed down from the wall and went back towards the castle gate. He knew he was taking an incredible risk. He had taken many risks in his lifetime, but all of them had been well thought out and calculated carefully beforehand. This risk was spontaneous which meant it was foolish, but he was beyond caring.

He strode rapidly until he reached the main gate. A guard stopped him.

"Identify yourself and your purpose," the guard demanded.

"I am Thomas Taylor from London." Roger lied. He blessed his good fortune that when they were in Grayton, Elaisse had told him about Fern. "I've come to visit my niece, Fern Carver. She is a servant inside the castle."

"Wait here," the guard instructed, and Roger was relieved that the man hadn't seemed to notice that he wasn't old enough to be the uncle of a grown woman.

After what seemed to be an exceedingly long time, the guard returned, leading a pretty young woman who had thick, reddish-brown hair and a mole on her left cheek. Fern looked at Roger with suspicion but said nothing. The guard hovered near them.

"How nice to see you, Fern," Roger said. "Are you taking good care of Elaisse?"

Fern's eyes seemed to light up as she recognized Roger as the man who had sat on the castle wall. "It's good to see you, Uncle. But I must get back to my duties. Perhaps if you stay in the village, I can visit you later."

"How much later?" Roger asked.

"It's hard to say, but I hope you will stay and wait," Fern told him, then she motioned to the guard and went back to the castle.

The guard remained at the gate, glaring at Roger.

"I'll take my leave now," Roger grinned and got on his horse.

««—»»

Elaisse was hiding in the servants' living quarters. Usually crowded with maids, cooks, grooms, stable hands, gardeners, valets, and other castle assistants, since the Great Dying it was almost empty.

When she saw the conditions in which the servants were expected to reside, she felt shame for her own family because she had always lived so well. In contrast, the servants' quarters were cramped, damp, and cold. Only a minimal amount of lighting was allowed, and it was windowless and dark. Vermin roamed freely because the castle rats seemed to reside in the basement where conditions were dark enough to hide them. Elaisse swore that if she ever got out of this situation, she would set poison for all the castle rats. After all she had seen them do, she despised rats.

Suddenly Fern came into the room. "I talked to Roger!"

"Does he know I am in hiding?"

"He told the guard he is my uncle. He must be clever," Fern said. "And yes, I think he knows you are hiding. I told him to wait in the village and I would try to bring word about you later."

And then Fern looked away, so Elaisse asked, "What?"

Fern looked back at Elaisse, meeting her eyes directly as she said, "I spied on Henry and John again. They know you've escaped from the wine cellar. Henry is furious."

"What are they doing to try to find me?"

"They've sent a guard into the woods to search for you. Another is in the village. And a third is on the road to London, seeking you there," Fern told her. "That means there are only two guards left here in the castle."

"I need to go to the village and meet Roger there."

"I know. I've already arranged with the villagers to provide you with a horse after the sun goes down. They will protect you."

"Why would the villagers cooperate with my escape? Why are they providing me with a horse at no cost?"

Fern said, "Elaisse, there is unrest among the villagers. It's an uprising happening all across England. The peasants are rebelling; they feel there should be changes to the working conditions. That's why the villagers are so willing to help you—they feel you would be more sympathetic to their cause than Henry."

"I'm grateful to them. And if I survive this, I will bring my brother to justice; not only for the murder of our mother, but for the abandonment of the villagers during the Great Dying. I'll leave after sundown. "

"Promise me you'll be careful! Henry is telling John that since you've escaped, now you need to be killed."

"I'll be careful. I need to succeed so I can make changes to the working conditions for the peasants." It didn't occur to Elaisse that she was already making plans to become the ruler of Wynham Castle.

When sunset came, Elaisse fidgeted with nerves. By the time twilight approached, she began pacing the stone floor. When the sky became fully engulfed in darkness, she was ready.

She wore a dark brown tunic, almost black, and a matching cloak so she would blend with the night. Her golden hair was tightly braided, pinned up to her head, and tucked under the hood of the dark cloak.

Fern had been exploring the castle, and said, "John is asleep in the guest room, but Henry is still up. He's drinking again in the dining hall. There's only one guard watching the castle, at the main doorway of the keep. But remember, there are other guards: one in the forest and another in the village."

"How will I get past the guard in the keep?" Elaisse asked.

"Leave it to me. That guard has had his eye on me for a long time," Fern said. "I'll splash myself with brandy so will think I've been drinking, then I'll flirt with him. He'll be occupied." Fern did as she said with the brandy, and then the two women stepped carefully into the hallway.

Elaisse's senses were heightened as adrenaline coursed through her veins. She felt that this must be what deer experienced as they roamed the forest—relying upon the instinctive primal sensations of sight, sound and scent to guide them and not intellect. Elaisse realized that she felt like a wild animal: hunted, and on the alert for predators. Except in her case, the predator was her brother, not a wolf.

Fern led the way down the stairs that would take them to the keep. The stairs were steep and slippery with groundwater that constantly leaked through the masonry walls. No thoughts for safety were considered when the stairs were built. They were much steeper and more precarious than those on the upper levels. Elaisse couldn't help but wonder how many servants had fallen down these dangerous steps.

They climbed up to the ground level. They continued up to the second story where the main castle door in the keep was located. Creeping stealthily and silently, the two women used hand signals to communicate.

They reached the exit hallway and Fern motioned to stop. She held up one finger in a gesture to wait. Elaisse hid in a wall crevice while Fern went on ahead to meet the guard. She stood waiting, hidden in the dark shadows.

Elaisse could hear conversation and listened for the key phrase that she and Fern had previously agreed upon. She knew that once the signal was given, she was to continue alone because Fern would be occupied.

There! She heard Fern utter the signal phrase. She could hear the voices receding as Fern led the guard away from his post. *Please God, protect Fern*, Elaisse prayed.

She peered out from her spot in the crevice. No one was in sight. She took a deep breath, then scampered to the main door of the keep and worked the pulleys that opened it.

The night air touched her face and she breathed the fresh fragrance deeply. She noticed that the moon was full; an unfortunate event because of the amount of light it gave. But she had no choice; she could not wait for the moon to wane and despite unfavorable conditions, this was the only night she had to escape.

She quickly went down the steps that were on the outside of

the castle. She knew that as long as she was on the stairs, she was vulnerable. She must make it to the ground.

Finally she reached the ground and raced across the meadow that appeared gray in the moonlight. She ran for the road that led to the village, knowing she would be in an open space and obvious if anyone cared to look in her direction.

After running a distance, she became winded and slowed herself to a walk. She tried to keep her panting breaths quiet, and was careful to step accurately and swiftly. It could be a disaster if she turned her ankle.

Reaching the village, she passed by the first of the cottages. She noticed how dark and deserted the village appeared, its population greatly thinned. Yet she couldn't shake the feeling that she was being watched.

She found Fern's cottage, and as she stood in front, her thoughts briefly turned to the boy Edward, now resting in the kitchen garden out back. She shook off the memory, and became determined to stay in the present, in the moment. It was a matter of life and death to do so.

Suddenly a shape materialized out of the dark night.

Elaisse turned to flee.

"Don't run!" came the voice of a young man. "I'm a friend, here to help you."

Elaisse knew she couldn't escape without a horse, so she turned to face the stranger. "Who are you?"

"I am Simon, from this village."

She looked at him as he stepped out of the night's gloom into the moonlight, and she saw he wasn't much older than poor Edward who was lying in the garden earth. "Do you have a horse for me?" she asked.

"Behind the cottage. Follow me."

He turned and she followed him around the dwelling, and a large black horse stood tethered at the kitchen garden. "When you escape," Simon said, "you must come back. This village needs your interference against your brother Henry. We believe you can make a difference in our lives."

"That I promise," Elaisse told him as she mounted the black horse.

"I'm going to walk ahead as a scout," Simon instructed. "Wait here ten minutes, then proceed back towards the castle. You will need to exit the main gate to reach the road to London. There will be another villager waiting for you on the other side of the gate. His name is Richard."

Then Simon disappeared into the moonlit night, almost as if he had never been there at all.

She silently counted the ten minutes. Her horse snorted and chomped at its bit, giving Elaisse the impression it was well rested and eager. Finally, convinced the ten minutes were up, she snapped at the reins and the horse bolted forward.

She headed for the castle. She knew she had to trust that her mount was sure-footed. She reached the gate, and found no guard there. She dismounted only long enough to work the pulleys to open the gate. She would have to leave it open, and she prayed no one would notice until morning.

She got back on her horse and rode through the gate to the open land beyond.

She heard a noise and another man stepped into view. "I am Richard from the village. My role is to shut the castle gate from the inside to buy you more time."

She breathed a sigh of relief that the gate would not be left open after all. "Thank you, Richard," she said. "Your service will not be forgotten."

"We're counting on that," Richard said as he slipped back into the castle grounds.

Elaisse snapped the reins again and her mount bolted forward. She rode at a frenzied gallop away from the castle. The brightness of the moon created conditions that allowed for faster travel since she could see so well. But if she could see, so could her enemies.

The shrubs and trees sped by and the wind threatened to blow her cowl off her head as Elaisse urged the horse on. The mount's mane whipped at her face as she leaned forward for minimal wind resistance. She could hear the horse's breaths as they blasted from its nostrils and she could feel the muscles tighten and loosen with every stretch of its legs.

Suddenly another rider burst out from behind a tree into the roadway directly in front of her. Elaisse reined her horse to a stop, hoping against hope that this was the promised villager and not a castle guard.

"Who goes there?" she called.

"I am Elden, to escort you to London," came the reply.

She felt relief, and peered at him. She could see him clearly in the moonlight, a man with long hair that was tied into a nape at his neck. Elden's head was bare of covering and his hair appeared dark gray in the moon's reflection. He was thin but had broad shoulders that probably came from hard labor in the fields. His horse was large and dark, similar to her own.

As Elaisse approached Elden, she was aware of a *whooshing* sound close to her ear.

She was momentarily confused; the sound seemed familiar but it came and went so fast that she was unable to identify it. For a second she was not even certain she had heard it at all.

And then she heard a strangled gargling sound, and she turned her head towards Elden, wondering what on earth he was doing. The villager was making strange sounds and he began to lean forward in his saddle.

"Elden!" she cried, alarmed. "What is it?"

His horse shied to the left and with that movement, Elden dropped off the animal and fell into a heap upon the ground. His horse snorted in surprise and turned around, trotting back towards the castle.

And in that moment, Elaisse knew. The long, straight rod protruding from Elden's throat confirmed her worst fears.

Someone had shot Elden with a large arrow, the type that could only be from a crossbow. Not many people knew how to use crossbows because they were a recent military invention.

But Henry knew.

And so she realized that Henry was pursuing her, and he had

deadly accuracy with the crossbow.

Panicked, Elaisse snapped at the reins and her horse bolted, but she managed to hold on. She heard another *whoosh* right by her ears. If she hadn't moved her horse that very second, the passing arrow would have found its mark in her flesh.

Urging her horse to run faster, she could hear hoofbeats thundering behind as Henry followed in pursuit. He would have to stop and dismount to use the crossbow, but she knew he was also an expert with the regular bow and arrow. And that could be used as he rode.

To become less of a target, Elaisse tried to stagger the direction in which her horse ran, but her mount resisted anything but a straightforward course. Spontaneously she turned her horse off the road and into the weeds and underbrush of the terrain that was unknown to her. She pushed her horse forward, trying to evade the trees and praying that her mount could avoid any animal holes in the ground.

Suddenly a deer burst from the underbrush and jumped directly in her path. Her horse was startled, and it stopped too abruptly for Elaisse to compensate. The horse reared up in a frightened reaction to the deer and she felt herself sliding backwards over the animal's hindquarters. She desperately tried to grab for the saddle in an attempt to pull herself back to a position of control, but missed.

Her horse bolted forward and she felt herself free-fall for seemingly endless moments until she hit the hardpan of the ground.

Winded, she gasped for breath but it was knocked out of her. She felt lightning bolts of pain shoot from her right elbow because she had used that arm to break her fall. She felt sick as she realized she was helpless to move. And she could hear a horse approaching rapidly.

She would never reach London. Henry would kill her.

And there was nothing she could do about it.

It was over.

Calm settled over her mind as she prepared to die. She

committed herself to God and felt oddly at peace. It was as though she was dreaming, and somehow she had the ability to be an impartial observer of the events unfolding in the wild terrain near the road to London.

Henry reached her and dismounted. He drew his military sword from his saddlebag. He let his horse go, throwing the reins over the mount's head to the ground. The horse understood that as a command to stay put.

"Well, dear Sister," he said. "You had your chance to see reason."

Elaisse sat up, but remained on the ground and said nothing. The pain in her elbow was receding.

Henry continued, "At one time, you could have been an asset to me, but you chose not to cooperate. Our father would be ashamed of you. Imagine choosing peasants over centuries of tradition! You deserve to die and I will take pleasure in feeding you to the wolves."

"First you must deal with me," came a voice from the bushes.

Elaisse turned her head in surprise. Roger! Where had he come from? How did he know?

Roger stepped out from the darkness of the underbrush, and the moonlight gleamed from his sword. Henry turned to face him, snarling in almost bestial intonation. Both men stood facing each other, sizing up the other, both holding their weapons in front of them, their swords pointing at the moon.

"Identify yourself so I know my opponent," Henry demanded.

"I am Roger Browne, loyal to the cause of Wat Tyler from Essex."

Elaisse gasped. So that was why he had always been so secretive.

"Roger Browne, you are a traitor to the throne," Henry accused. "Prepare to die."

Henry rushed at Roger, who met him halfway. The intense clanging of the swords as they connected reverberated through the night, and the flash of metal in the moonlight was almost illuminating.

Elaisse stood up, wanting to help Roger, but the two men moved so quickly with their feints and lunges that she didn't know how to effectively interfere. Every other minute the two swords connected loudly as one man moved to block the other's thrusts.

The moonlight reflected upon the scene that was unfolding, and Elaisse could clearly witness the fight in front of her. Neither man was dressed for battle. Neither wore protection so if one of the blades were to reach its target, it meant certain death for the victim.

She felt helpless because the men moved so quickly, it would be impossible to help without fatally distracting the wrong man. So she tried to stay back but was unable to help herself. She had to do *something*.

She ran for Henry's horse, and searched his saddlebag. There! A large knife.

Elaisse yanked the knife out of the saddlebag and raced back to where the men were still in the swordfight. Where she had cursed the bright moonlight earlier, now she blessed her ability to see which man was which.

She slowly approached her brother, making sure Roger could see she was there. Henry was concentrating on his swordsmanship, and was unaware that his sister was sneaking up behind him.

Elaisse held the knife above her shoulders, and then thrust it down with all her strength. Images of stabbing an intruder in Thomas Taylor's London tenement flashed before her eyes, but this time it was her own brother whom she stabbed.

Putting her entire weight into her thrust, the knife connected with Henry's back, penetrating between the shoulder blades. Tearing into the flesh, only the bones of the ribcage stopped the blow from being fatal.

But she had the element of surprise in her favor, and as her brother stiffened with pain, Roger drove his own sword deep into Henry's stomach and twisted the weapon.

In what seemed to be endless minutes of slow motion, Henry

remained standing, jerking with convulsions. Then he dropped silently to the ground. In the moonlight, the pool of blood which seeped into the earth around his body appeared black as coal.

Both Elaisse and Roger stood above the dead man, panting with exertion. Finally Elaisse spoke. "I've killed my own brother."

"Not everything that is necessary is easy," he told her and took her in his arms. "You didn't kill him by yourself. We did what we had to do and we did it together."

She buried her face in his chest. "I know."

"I can tell you that by this man's death, many others will live," Roger said. "And they will live as people and not as slaves. Throughout history, horses have been treated better than peasants. But that was the old way. Wat Tyler's movement is a series of small steps. Henry is the last of the old ways at Wynham Castle. Build upon his downfall to make a better world that Wat Tyler wants us to have."

Elaisse spoke into Roger's chest, her voice muffled. "Not everything will simply fall into place. A man named John Wythe has come back from the war in France. He will want to convict me for Henry's death so he can control the castle. I need to convince him otherwise, and not by killing him. I don't want any more bloodshed."

She lifted her head and looked up at him. "We need to give Henry a Christian burial. He needs prayers for forgiveness."

"I think we should leave his body for the forest scavengers," Roger said.

"No, I have a more just plan. I want my brother buried in the village, in a kitchen garden behind a cottage. Henry will be buried next to a fourteen-year-old boy who died of the pestilence. I want Henry's body laid next to a peasant as a symbol of one man's equality to another, regardless of the differences of lineage."

Chapter Sixteen

In the village next to Wynham Castle, the rats that once lived in the thatched roofs of the cottages had long perished. Most of the pigs had also expired, as they lived alongside the humans inside the houses. The village dogs were sick and dying.

In the fields outside the castle walls, sheep began to die. Because the villagers were more concerned with the continuing deaths of their own family members, the decline in the sheep herd went almost unnoticed. With no one to remove the bodies from the fields, the sheep simply rotted where they fell. Sheep that were not yet sick walked away from the grazing meadows to wind up wherever they chose to roam.

All these deaths, yet many of the fleas that carried *Yersinia pestis* bacteria still lived.

The wandering sheep carried the fleas all over the countryside. In turn, wild animals contracted fleas that fled from the dying sheep.

John Wythe took one of the castle's falcon s to hunt in the forest outside the wall He knew the village livestock had sickened and he wanted fresh meat, so he decided to seek wild game.

John became troubled and even anxious when he entered the forest because of the seemingly disproportionate number of dead squirrels that lay scattered throughout the underbrush.

Seeing that death had come here too, John lost his appetite for fresh meat and didn't touch the falcon's hood, so the bird was never released from his wrist. He spoke softly to the falcon to calm her, and then turned to leave the forest.

As he headed in the direction of Wynham Castle, John was unaware that an infected flea had leapt upon his ankle.

Early to Mid-June 1349

John Wythe tossed and turned in the elaborate bed that was in one of the castle's guest bedrooms. His temperature was elevated, and the linen sheets were soaked with rancid sweat. He knew it was late, after midnight, and that he should feel tired. But his nerves felt jittery and one of his legs kept twitching.

A sudden wave of nausea threatened to overwhelm him, but he gulped great breaths of air to calm his system. John reached for a mug of water by his bedside and drank it down. Immediately he realized that it was a mistake, for his stomach revolted against the liquid. John barely had enough time to rush his face over the side of the bed so that the steaming, caustic vomit would become a projectile onto the floor and not onto the bed.

Eventually reduced to dry heaves, he lay back, prone upon the bed. He knew he should summon a maid to clean up the mess he made on the floor, but he couldn't seem to find the strength to care.

From the back corners of his mind, ideas tried to invade his psyche about the likelihood that he had contracted the pestilence. But in the forefront of his mind, he dismissed that possibility. He consoled himself with the fact that he had been sick many times in his life and had always recovered. He told himself that this was just another one of those times.

John knew there was one way to be sure. He had only to feel his groin or underneath his armpits for the truth. But he was afraid; he didn't want to be *that* certain about his illness. So he pointedly avoided those areas of his body that might reveal the telltale buboes.

While he had been delirious with fever earlier, now he was experiencing a phase of lucidity. He could think clearly. He clung to the hope that it meant the worst was past him.

During this period of clarity, he began to reminisce about his life.

He had been given the title of knight because of the public display of bravery during jousting matches when he had demonstrated seemingly superior qualities. But when he went to France, he was faced with the violence of real war. Suddenly he had realized the difference between pretend and reality.

He was overwhelmed on the battlefield when he understood that there, the intentions of his opponents were not to play games, but to actually kill him. He had known fear for the first time in his life, and was surprised that his reaction to fear was to avoid it. John maneuvered to never lead the regiments and always surrounded himself with braver men.

When the Great Dying made it obvious that the war in France could no longer continue, John used it as an opportunity to run away. He couldn't help himself. He was overcome because he was faced with two deadly enemies: the French and the pestilence.

And so he became a deserter. John knew that with all the confusion of the Great Dying, no one would realize that he was running away like the coward he was.

He thought of Elaisse. Had he ever loved her? Certainly he had been attracted to her. In his own way, perhaps he did love her. But when he thought back to the time before the world fell apart, he had trouble remembering her.

Elaisse! If only she had married him. That was impossible now, because certainly Henry had caught and killed her by this time of night. He had so badly wanted the title the marriage would have given him that he almost salivated over it.

Now it was not going to happen.

John's fever began rising once again and he began to sweat. He felt thirsty but couldn't remember if he had already drunk the mug of water by his bed or not. He was dimly aware of the scent of vomit in the room but had no idea of why the smell would be there. Gradually he drifted back into delirium.

«« — »»

The guard met them at the main gate. "Who goes there?"

Elaisse identified herself. Roger rode alongside her, and led the third horse with Henry's dead body draped over it. The guard showed undisguised surprise when he recognized the remains of the duke of Wynham Castle.

Elaisse thought, *What can the guard do?* She knew the guard understood that the affairs of state would now lie in her hands, and her hands alone.

And so the guard made no comment as he opened the gate to them.

Roger led Henry's horse to the stable, where he carefully lifted the body and placed it on the ground inside. Since no servants came to assist, Elaisse and Roger worked side-by-side to remove saddles and put the horses into empty stalls.

"We'll bury Henry in the morning," Roger said, then looked at her. "What now? Do you want me to go with you inside the castle or should I leave?"

Elaisse smiled. "You mean now I have a choice as to whether you leave me or not?"

He grinned back at her. "Ouch. I guess I deserved that one."

"Well, what do you say to that?"

"I could tell you I will never leave you again, but I would prefer to show you. Don't forget I know where a priest is hiding. He could marry us tonight."

"Oh, I'll marry you all right, just not tonight," she said. "The problems for this night are not yet over; we still have to face John Wythe. I may need your help."

He took her hand and together they strolled in the moonlight towards the castle. The night was warm and hinted of summer. The crickets and frogs were in full chorus, and a screech owl searched noisily for the rodents that were now very scarce.

Elaisse thought, *Somehow nature will find a way to continue past the Great Dying, and perhaps mankind will also find a way.*

They climbed the outside stairs of the castle in a single file,

Elaisse in the lead. They entered the castle, and Roger looked around.

"Such grandeur," he commented icily.

"You'll get used to it," she told him.

"Elaisse, all of this wealth comes from back-breaking peasant labor," he scolded. "For centuries, England has been a country of slaves and masters, of haves and have-nots, all as a result of serfdom."

She stopped in the passageway, and whirled to face him. The torchlight revealed the anger on her face. "I'm aware of your politics! And although I believe the government has been wrong all these centuries, I believe your methods for change are also wrong. There has to be a compromise. There has to be something that would be fair for everybody."

As he always did at inappropriate times, Roger laughed. "How I love such a spirited lady!"

"Oh, you are so contrary!" But she was accustomed to him by now, and his manner no longer bothered her. She realized that oftentimes his laughter served to break the tension.

And Elaisse thought, *Perhaps I could learn something from Roger. After all, he has heard what the peasants are saying, and I have not yet heard them speak.* But she remained quiet on the subject, because this was no time to stage a debate. There were more pressing matters to deal with first.

The couple passed through the castle to the higher floors, and she could feel his hand tighten on hers. When they reached her room, Elaisse asked Roger to wait in the hallway.

She entered the room quietly; stealthily. She tip-toed across the room, searching. And as she suspected, she saw Fern sleeping on the bed.

Gingerly Elaisse touched Fern's cheek to make sure she was alive and well. Feeling the healthy warmth from her skin, Elaisse became convinced of her friend's safety. She turned to leave the room, thinking it better not to disturb Fern until morning, which would be soon enough. Dawn was breaking.

She went back into the passageway where Roger waited and

whispered, "I'll show you to an empty guest room."
"Will you join me there?" he asked.
"Only for an hour. But it will be such a nice hour."

Chapter Seventeen

The mortality caused by the bubonic plague between 1346 and 1350 was the worst demographic disaster in the history of the world to this date. In less than four years, the disease carved a path of death through Asia, Italy, France, North Africa, Spain and Normandy, made its way over the Alps into Switzerland, and continued eastward into Hungary. After a brief respite, the plague resumed, crossing the channel into England, Scotland, and Ireland. Eventually, the plague made its way into the northern countries of Norway, Sweden, Denmark, Iceland and even as far north as Greenland.

It seemed there was no one unaffected by the "pestilence." King Edward III's favorite daughter Joanna died of the plague while on her way to Bordeaux to marry Pedro of Castile.

And afterwards, the declining population of workers created a need for new methods of production that required less manpower. It was a time of inventions, and it became a brave new world.

Society changed, finding time to develop the arts. Accomplished artists emerged and their creations began to look away from the morbid works of the plague years into a new brightness of beauty. The ending of the medieval "dark ages" led to the enlightenment of the Renaissance Period.

Mid to Late June 1349

The guard who was surprised to see Henry's body pass through the gate had time to think about it. He was now furious. His name was Walter and he had enjoyed the immense salary that Henry paid him to work at the castle during the frightening time of widespread sickness.

When he opened the gate for Elaisse Sheffield and the body of his former employer, Walter instinctively understood that no one would pay him the amount of money that Henry had ever again.

It was not that Walter had any affection for Henry. It was not as though he admired the man. Instead, Walter felt that Elaisse cheated him out of a very good wage by killing her brother.

And so he decided to abandon his post at the main gate. Since he knew the amount of his salary would change, he no longer felt compelled to stay. Walter went back to the village, where he began to drink.

Towards dawn, Walter was very drunk. His degree of anger increased with his degree of drunkenness.

It was then that Walter decided he would ride to London to see revenge on Elaisse Sheffield. Walter would tell the authorities that Elaisse should be investigated for the murder of her own brother.

«« —»»

Elaisse woke in a rarely used guest room, alone, having left Roger's room hours ago. She realized that she had slept later than she wanted, so she sat up with a start. She remembered Fern, and wanted to make sure everything was all right. Quickly she dressed and left the room.

When she reached the bedroom of her childhood, at first Elaisse thought the room was empty. But a second later, Fern crawled out from underneath the bed.

"What on earth were you doing down there?" Elaisse asked.

"I'm so glad it's you! I was hiding because I was afraid it was Henry."

"You don't have to be afraid of Henry anymore. He's dead."

Fern looked relieved. "I know it is terrible to think such thoughts, but I'm not sad about that."

Elaisse noticed that Fern asked no questions, and she didn't volunteer any answers. Instead, Elaisse asked, "Can you make a shroud for my brother? I'd sew it myself, but there's something else I need to do. Oh, and one more thing—you're free to go anywhere you want in this castle now. There's no need to hide anymore. Remember, you are not a servant, you are my friend."

She paused, and then added, "Have you seen John Wythe?"

"Not for about two days," Fern said.

"Well, I'd better find him before he finds me." She went back into the passageway.

She reached the main guest quarters where she knew John had been staying. Tentatively she knocked on the door, but there was no response.

She rapped louder, and heard a groan from within. Alarmed, she shouted through the door, "John! Are you all right?"

There was no response.

The modesty of the times dictated that a woman could not enter a man's bedroom by herself. The rules did not allow Elaisse to enter a man's room who was not her husband. But she knew something was wrong inside that room. What to do?

She went to Roger's room and knocked. The door swung open and his eyes lit up when he saw her. "I need your help," she told him.

Together they went to John's room. Roger opened the door and was repelled by the stench of vomit. But Elaisse recognized the scent as not just vomit, but the pestilence. She remembered how it smelled when she nursed her mentor, Thomas Taylor back in London. Would the sickness that invaded the land ever end?

John lay on the bed, his body feverish and twitching.

"The *danse macabre*," Roger said.

"Poor John. He doesn't deserve this," Elaisse said, and Roger agreed, not knowing that once upon a time, John had been his competition for Elaisse's love.

"I'll help you clean up," Roger said. "I don't think you'll find any servants to do it."

Elaisse stopped for a moment to look at him. It was not a man's job to see to the ill. Tradition said that was a chore for women only. Yet there was nothing traditional about Roger, so unlike Henry and yes, so unlike even John. She loved Roger for his rebellions as to what society dictated. Roger was flexible, and could change with changing times. She needed to change too.

"Can you find a bucket and washrag?" she asked. "I'll stay with John."

Normally a man would not be expected to fetch anything either, but Roger left to complete the chore.

With Roger gone, Elaisse took a linen kerchief from the dresser drawer and sat in a chair next to John's bed. She used the cloth to wipe his forehead. She was surprised when John opened his eyes.

He was surprisingly coherent. "Elaisse! I was so afraid that Henry killed you."

Then he said, "I can't seem to stop twitching."

"Relax," she soothed. "Here, let me wipe your forehead again."

"Elaisse, I need to talk to you."

"Not now. You don't need to talk now."

"Yes I do," he said. "I have to talk now, because I think I am going to die."

He was right, he was going to die. They both knew it and she was glad that she didn't have to pretend otherwise.

"I need to know what my life meant," he said. "What was my purpose for living?"

She took his hand, partly to comfort him, and partly to calm the twitching. "I don't think that is for any of us to know."

"I need to confess. The Bishops said we could confess to a woman."

"I'll listen."

"I've made so many mistakes," he said, "and done things I regret. Look at the things I did to you. I should never have tried to force you to love me. I should have made myself more loveable instead."

"I am fine with you just as you are. Don't worry about my feelings, because I understand all that you did and I am not upset. In another land, in another time, everything you did would have been appropriate. It's not your fault that everything changed overnight. You need to be able to forgive yourself."

John sighed, then said, "I was thinking so much about the future that I forgot about the present. Because of that, I wound up living my life in neither the future nor the present. Now the future will never come for me, and I wasted the present."

Elaisse said nothing, but continued to hold his hand and occasionally wiped the sweat from his brow. It was the talk of the dying, from someone who had to make peace with his own soul.

He went on, "Now that I am so near to death, I feel like I almost know something. I'm close to understanding a great mystery. Before I was always 'too busy.' But by stopping the distractions of life's everyday routines, I have the time to evaluate more spiritual things. I am finally in the present, *in the now.*"

He paused to think, then continued, "It's like when you clean the dust off of something, you can discover what lies underneath. I've cleaned the dust of ambition and greed off myself, and what lies underneath is exposed. Now that I'm on my death bed, I am not thinking about any titles or any other symbols of status. I am thinking that you were right all along: that caring about others is what gives life meaning. "

She let him talk. She let him cleanse his soul.

"There's so much explained with nature," he said. "Many plants die back every winter, but come back again in the spring. That's how nature lives eternally. Why can't I die now and come back to live again in the spring? I suppose I must leave to make room for new babies who will try their own luck in the world."

A tear rolled down his cheek that was ravaged by disease. "And so now I must die. I do so with the realization that to be rich is not determined by who has the most, but by who can be happy with the least. So many people are seekers in life—they seek happiness so laboriously that they spend all their time chasing after their mistaken belief in things that could bring them that happiness. But real happiness is intangible. And intangible things are invisible unless people look within themselves. People can travel, to get away from what they perceive is causing their dissatisfaction. I tried it by going to France. But wherever I went, I always took me with me. I was never happy with myself, so I always tried to validate myself by external things. Now I see that the old saying 'happiness comes from within' is true."

He drifted for a moment, then said, "Now that I'm actually doing it, I suppose dying is not as frightening as I would have imagined. I feel a sense of serenity because for the first time, I know myself. With this knowledge comes a clarity of thought; a sense of spirituality. There is a design much greater than me as an individual. That design is nature, which will always continue. After my death, plants will come back every spring. Life goes on. And I'm so glad it will, because nature is where God must be. Today I am already spiritually part of nature, and after I am laid into the ground to decompose, I will become physically part of nature. Only then will I be one with God."

She waited for John to continue talking, but instead his leg jerked, and his eyes began to wander. When she was sure he would not speak again, Elaisse wiped his forehead and began talking soothingly to him. She told him meaningless things, like how everything would turn out all right. She knew he was taking comfort from the sound of her voice, and that he did not have to die all alone.

Was that what life was really all about, that no one should be alone, that they should have friends and family; someone to care about them? Or was that what John was referring to when he said we should not receive validation from external things? Were other people external things?

Perhaps instead, John had hit more on the truth when he said we should make ourselves more lovable. Perhaps instead of worrying about others caring for us, perhaps we should care for others. Elaisse understood that when she helped others, it seems to lessen her own problems. It took her out of herself and made life better not only for the ones she was helping, but her own life as well. And that was why she needed to make changes in society. Others needed her help.

Her mind wandered to the previous night, when she had been sure she was going to die by Henry's hand. She vividly recalled crouching on the ground, waiting for the fell swoop of the sword that would penetrate her flesh and end her life.

She remembered the odd sense of serenity when she made peace with herself to accept death. She had been so calm.

But now that death was no longer a threat, she could not bring back that feeling of serenity. Now that she was granted a second chance at life, she could not retrieve that feeling of inner peace that had enveloped her when she was so close to death.

Maybe that is as it should be, she thought. Perhaps the business of living was to live, and not to dwell on death.

But still, she knew her experience with near-death had somehow changed her; she was enlightened as to a greater awareness of the little things in life, whether it was to notice a bee on a flower, or an appreciation of a warm, sunny day.

Elaisse wanted to learn something from all this death surrounding her. She figured John was telling her to set aside some time every day to stop and contemplate the now; to meditate on simply being. She needed to view life differently, to appreciate each moment, and to give it a new value.

And then Roger entered the room, carrying a bucket and a wash rag. He came next to John's bed and looked at the dying man. Roger did not ask for Elaisse's assessment of John's condition; there was no need.

Neither Roger nor Elaisse spoke as he got down on the floor to clean the vomit. Elaisse went back to the dresser to retrieve linen and thread.

She sat in the chair by the bed, keeping vigil, and humming softly as she sewed John's shroud.

«« — »»

There was a knock on the door. Roger rose and opened it, and Fern stood in the hallway.

"There's someone who wants to see both of you," Fern said.

"Can it wait?" Roger asked.

"No...I think you'd better come now," Fern said.

Elaisse put down her sewing. She glanced at John Wythe, but he was deep in coma, unaware of his surroundings. She supposed he would not miss her at this point if she left his side.

Fern led them to the main door of the castle keep. She told them that someone was waiting outside at the bottom of the steps. It was all very mysterious, because Fern seemed upset and didn't want to talk.

Elaisse could see someone standing at the base of the steps, holding something that was unclear to her. As she maneuvered the steps until she was close to the ground, she suddenly recognized the person as Simon, the young man from the village cottage who had given her the horse at the kitchen garden.

She reached the ground and suddenly realized what Simon was holding.

It was the head of a man. Simon was holding the head by its hair.

The skin was bleached white from blood loss, and its hair was stringy and matted. The eyes were partially opened to reveal milky orbs, the nose was crusted with dried blood, and the tongue protruded from the mouth. The head had been cut off at the throat, and twisted sinews of muscle, veins, and ligaments were visible from the severed neck.

After everything she had seen in the Great Dying, after nursing three dying people with their putrid illnesses, and even after chancing upon dead corpses eaten by rats or rotting in decomposition; she was still not prepared for what she was seeing now.

She turned around and ran a few paces, then knelt upon the grassy ground and vomited. Both Roger and Simon waited patiently for her nausea to pass, neither commenting or even acknowledging that she was losing the contents of her stomach.

When she was able to steady herself, Elaisse wiped her mouth on her sleeve. Then she rose and walked back to where Simon was waiting, patiently holding the severed human head.

"Who is it?" Elaisse said, getting to the point of what she

wanted to know.

Simon answered, "This is Walter Miller. Your brother recently appointed him as castle guard. Last night, Walter was in the village, very drunk. He was bragging that he would seek revenge upon you for the death of Sir Henry."

Elaisse did not recognize Walter Miller, but it was probably because he hadn't looked like this when he had let her into the gate. "So this guard intended to carry out his threat?"

"My Lady," Simon said, "we caught him two miles out on the road to London early this morning. His death is justified."

"Why is his death justified?"

"Because this man was going to destroy the villager's opportunity for a better life," Simon explained. "We had a meeting last night. We decided that Sir Henry's fate was none of our business, and that our only concern is for the welfare of the peasants as a collective."

"So you collectively decided to protect me," Elaisse said. "What do you want in return?"

"We want to be recognized as human beings. We want to be able to keep enough of the crops to feed our families. We want ownership of some of the land, or at least, fairer rents on the land the castle owns. We want to be able to trade freely. We want better living conditions for our children."

Elaisse told him, "Right now my first concern is to pay for clean up, sanitation, police, and priests. We will consecrate new ground for the burial of your loved ones, and not burn them. Once that is done, I will review your requests and do all I can to meet them. Of this I promise. Now, dispose of that head."

"My Lady," Simon bowed and walked away, and Elaisse knew she was in a position where she belonged.

She turned to Roger. "I will start on these things tomorrow. Today I have to bury my brother."

Epilogue

They married in the village church, with the blessing of the new priest, and the wedding was attended by everyone who wanted to attend. It was a new beginning, not only for Elaisse and Roger, but for the villagers who had never previously been invited to a marriage of a couple from the upper class.

She suspected she was pregnant; and she had told no one but Roger and Fern at this early stage. She was comforted by the fact that among all this dying, a new life would arrive. So perhaps what John Wythe had said about plants dying in winter only to come back again in the spring could apply to the human race as well.

She was keeping her promise to the villagers, and they in turn kept theirs. There were still a lot of negotiations to be done, but in Wynham, both sides were communicating.

Elaisse understood that right after the wedding, Roger would take a trip to London to meet with his group of government protestors. But she knew that he would come back to her, just as he had always come back.

Roger kissed the bride, then took her hand to lead her from the church. People threw flower petals at the newly married couple.

Author's Note about Creative Liberties

There were incidences of plague occurring and reoccurring throughout history, but this book focuses on the time period between 1346 through 1350. Although there was some plague in Russia in 1351, the disease had mostly run its course by then.

There really were "plague doctors," who were medical men trained in the superstitions of their time, which included the belief that wearing a bird-like mask (the beak filled with fragrant herbs and flowers) could ward off the "miasmas" of bad air.

However, these doctors existed during a separate devastating bubonic plague pandemic that occurred in the 17th Century, and not during the 14th Century outbreak that this book focuses upon.

The "plague doctor" garments were invented by Charles de L'Orme in 1619; they were first used in Paris, but later spread to be used throughout Europe. The protective suit consisted of a heavy fabric overcoat that was waxed, a mask of glassed eye openings and a cone shaped like a beak to hold scented substances.

So the mention of a "plague doctor" in *Pestilence: A Medieval Tale of Plague* is a creative liberty because these practitioners did not exist until the 1600s, but today are commonly associated with the bubonic plague in general, so I included one (briefly) in this book.

The next creative liberty was to condense the plague into one type. In reality there were three different types of plague in 1346-1350: the bubonic as described in this book which was the most common type; the pneumonic, spread by coughs and sneezes which was less common; and the septicemia, spread by bodily fluids such as blood, which was uncommon.

In this book I also took liberties with the mention of the priest

John Ball and the peasant Wat Tyler. Although these were both real people and they did the things described in this book, they did not encounter the events that I outlined for them until 1381.

Below is a history of England's peasant uprising, written by Michael Brown of Springfield, Missouri, and permission for reprinting was granted by the American Professional Services.

Michael Brown writes:

The Court of Common Pleas (the civil court, as opposed to the Court of King's Bench, the criminal court) decided early in the 14th Century that it "didn't have time for the affairs of peasants." The peasants immediately recognized that they had no rights enforceable by law.

By 1340 the judges in England had become so enamored with their own procedural technicalities that civil disputes languished for years. The English Parliament enacted a statute that year which allowed the Commissioners to move the judges aside and adjudicate their own cases.

In 1348 the Black Plague reached England. As many as half the people in the country died. The feudal lords, short of tenants, tried to make those remaining work even harder. Most of the people in England were treated no better than animals.

The common people had another barrier in their quest for rights. All English court documents from 1066 A.D. were written in what today is called "law French." Most of the men who could teach the language were dead of the Plague.

In 1381 the effort to strictly enforce the collection of taxes created discontent throughout England. Wat Tyler's rebellion was ignited when a tax collector tried to make a determination that Wat Tyler's daughter was of taxable age (15) by stripping her naked and assaulting her.

Tyler, who was working close by, heard the screams of his wife and daughter. He came running and smashed the tax collector's skull with a hammer.

For this act, he was cheered by his neighbors, and the commoners of the western division of Kent were brought together by his courage. Wat Tyler was elected their leader.

Wat Tyler's group joined another group led by two itinerant priests named John Ball and Jack Straw, and rose 100,000 strong to invade London. The enraged mob broke open every prison and beheaded every judge and lawyer they could capture.

They surrounded Richard II, who asked them what they wanted. Wat Tyler's answer was: "We will be free forever, our heirs and our lands."

Richard II agreed.

But in a face-to-face meeting with Wat Tyler a short time later, Richard II ordered the Lord Mayor of London to "set hands on him." Wat Tyler was stabbed through the throat with a short sword, and, as he lay writhing in agony on the ground after falling from his horse, he was stabbed through the belly.

Watching from a distance, the peasants instantly arranged themselves in order to do battle with their longbows. Richard II rode up to them and said, "Wat Tyler was a traitor." Confused, the peasants paused until soldiers arrived and dispersed the crowd.

Minus their (real) leader, the peasants went home. Richard II reneged on his promises and hanged 1,500 of the rebels after 'jury trials.' Those trials were presided over by Judge John Tresilian, who threatened the jurors in each trial that they too would be hanged if they didn't vote to convict.

Tresilian was himself hanged seven years later.

Richard II was forced to abdicate in 1399.

In closing, I will say that there are many great non-fiction books about the 14th Century outbreak of plague that are written in interesting and very readable formats. Two of my favorites are *The Black Death* by Philip Ziegler and *The Black Death, Natural and Human Disaster in Medieval Europe* by Robert S. Gottfried. If *Pestilence: A Medieval Tale of Plague* has given you an interest in the bubonic plague's influence on history, then I highly recommend both of those books.

2012
Jeani Rector, Editor
The Horror Zine
www.thehorrorzine.com

About the Author

While most people go to Disneyland while in Southern California, Jeani Rector went to the Fangoria Weekend of Horror there instead. She grew up watching the Bob Wilkins Creature Feature on television and lived in a house that had the walls covered with framed Universal Monsters posters. It is all in good fun and actually, most people who know Jeani personally are of the opinion that she is a very normal person. She just writes abnormal stories. Doesn't everybody?

Jeani Rector is the founder and editor of The Horror Zine and has had her stories featured in magazines such as *Aphelion, Midnight Street, Strange Weird and Wonderful, Dark River Press, Macabre Cadaver, Ax Wound, Horrormasters, Morbid Outlook, Horror in Words, Black Petals, 63Channels, Death Head Grin, Hackwriters, Bewildering Stories, Ultraverse,* and others.

The Horror Zine Books also offers

A Feast of Frights from The Horror Zine

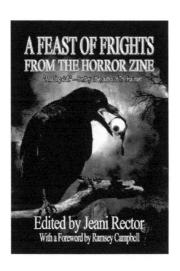

From the pages of The Horror Zine—the critically acclaimed online horror magazine—comes A FEAST OF FRIGHTS FROM THE HORROR ZINE. Featuring dark fantasy, mystery, pure suspense and classic horror, this book from The Horror Zine is relentless in its approach to basic fears and has twisted, unexpected endings. Come and find out what terrifying things can creep out of The Horror Zine to make your skin crawl.

"I have seen the future of horror—and so has Jeani Rector. In fact, she's publishing it. The Horror Zine books are not only fantastic reads, but they provide a valuable public service, exposing the world to up-and-coming talent in fiction, poetry, and art. Amazing stuff."
— Bentley Little, author of *The Haunted*

Made in the USA
Lexington, KY
22 June 2012